Small Town Love

Small Town Love

A Paradise Key Romance

Susan Meier

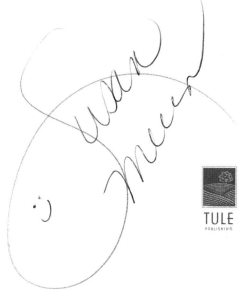

TULE
PUBLISHING

Chapter One

PHILADELPHIA, PENNSYLVANIA HAD a heartbeat.

Evelyn Barclay felt the pulse as she walked up the street to the Shutto Building, home of the offices of WKPP where she did a daily talk show. Taxi, bus, and car engines purred. High heels clicked. Conversations ebbed and flowed around her, as people bobbed along the sidewalk.

A few feet from her destination, she began inching to the right, easing out of the muddle of nine-to-fivers and into the cocooned doorway of her building. One quick push on the revolving door set it in motion. In three steps, she was in the lobby, waiting for an elevator with another group of people, this one quieter and impatient to get to their offices. The elevator came, she piled in, and the car began to ascend.

The woman beside her gave her a puzzled look, then her expression turned to one of recognition. Evelyn smiled at her. As the on-air talent for Philadelphia's biggest talk show, she was on *Live at Noon* five days a week. Her picture decorated the sides of buses and the backs of park benches.

A man in front turned and studied her. Evie smiled at him, too. She served at the pleasure of her audience, and she knew it.

The elevator stopped at her floor. As she stepped out, an older man called, "See you at noon."

Laughing at his use of the catch phrase for her show, she turned and winked. "See you at noon."

Everyone chuckled as the elevator door closed.

She sucked in a long, happy breath, so glad to be home she was almost giddy from it. She'd spent the past few months arriving at the crack of dawn every Monday morning to tape a week's worth of shows in one day before jetting back to Paradise Key, Florida and her childhood "posse" as they mourned the loss of their friend Lily.

She'd needed the time with them, but she'd missed Philadelphia. After being raised by a philandering dad, who'd sent her to boarding school and to Paradise Key for summer vacation, Evie had longed for a place to call home. A move ten years ago from Connecticut to Philadelphia had given her that home—and an identity she could be proud of. *This* was where she belonged.

WKPP took up three entire floors of the building, so the front desk was just beyond the elevator.

She walked up to the receptionist. "Good morning, Tilly."

"Ms. Barclay!" Curly-haired Tilly Franklin bounced out of her seat behind the tall counter. "Good morning! I didn't know you were coming in today. Nobody put it on my sheet!"

"I'm back for good now." She paused and laughed. "Except for vacations."

"It's nice to have you home."

"Thanks."

With a quick toss of her blond hair, Evie straightened the navy-blue blazer over her blue flowered silk sheath and headed to her office. With the actual studios and dressing rooms on a private floor, the corridor led to a section that housed advertising and marketing, cubicles where producers and their staffs scurried to make every WKPP program memorable, and finally the corridor to the offices of executive staff.

She strode into her suite, entering her secretary Janine's office. Janine came to attention. "Good morning!"

Evie picked up the stack of mail from the corner of her desk. "Good morning."

"How was Florida?"

"Better this time." She smiled at Janine. "My friends and I realized we were recovering from our loss. I promised to spend a week there every summer and a weekend or two every couple of months just for fun. Now I'm resuming real life. I won't be going to Florida again until the first weekend in August."

"You're back for good?" Janine's eye sort of twitched as she nudged her head in the direction of Evie's office. The door was closed, but she'd assumed that was because she'd been gone all week.

"Yes. Why?"

Janine leaned across the desk and whispered, "Mr. Tanner is in your office."

Equally quiet, Evelyn replied, "Really?" Excitement bubbled inside her. Marty Tanner loved giving good news. Reveled in it. The only reason he'd be in her office, waiting for her return, would be to welcome her back. Maybe to offer her a raise? Or maybe it was time for stock options? She'd worked hard. Hadn't complained. Been a team player. Even taping her shows rather than doing them live, the ratings had gone up. She was the star of this network. She never took it for granted, but she sure as heck had worked hard to get here.

Stock options were definitely in order.

She sucked in a breath, straightening her shoulders. "Hold my calls."

Janine gave her a thumbs-up signal.

Balanced on stilettos dyed to match the lightest flowers in her dress, she marched to her office door. With one quick twist of the knob, she opened it.

"Good morning, Marty."

He stood with his back to her, staring out at the magnificent Philadelphia skyline. Short and stout, but with a bloodline as rich as her own, he turned from the window.

"Evelyn."

His use of her full name and rough tone stopped her in her tracks. He motioned to one of the seats in front of her desk, then sat in the tall-back leather chair that had been in

Evelyn's family since her great-grandfather negotiated deals for coal and steel in the western side of the state.

Her good mood plummeted. So much for thinking she'd be getting stock options.

She ambled over, sliding the shoulder strap of her black briefcase down her arm and setting it on her desk.

"What can I do for you?"

He leaned back in her seat in the kind of power play that made her nerves jump. "We got word last night from an impeccable source that your dad is being arrested this morning for SEC violations."

She sank to the chair in front of her desk. "What?"

"When the news breaks, we expect you'll be hounded by everybody from the national news media to our own Charlie Johnson, who'll want an exclusive by the way."

Her head spun, a million things popping into her brain. After her mom and grandfather were killed in a plane crash, her dad had been the worst father in the world. He'd cheated, lied, and stolen from her trust fund. It didn't surprise her that he'd violated SEC regulations. But she'd spent a decade distancing herself from him. What happened to her dad should mean nothing to her.

Did mean nothing to her.

"I'm not the one being arrested."

"No. But you'll be the story. Or at least a big chunk of it. And you know WKPP's policy. Talent cannot be the story. We've already lined up replacements. You're off the air until this thing clears. Either when he pleads guilty and stops being news, or at the end of his trial."

Her heart plummeted. "The end of his trial? It could take a year for this to get to court!"

"And we don't want you sitting in a hot seat every day with your fans phoning in questions about your dad rather than the city."

"I could handle them! I could tell people I'm troubled by my father's arrest, but remind them he and I are estranged. Then I'll wish him well with the proceedings. And we'll go on as normal."

Marty shook his head as if he thought she was crazy. "This won't go away with a wave of your wealthy Jones/Barclay magic wand. Your grandfather's been dead for twenty years. His charisma might have lingered in the minds of the last generation, but it doesn't mean squat to the new one. To them, he is a rich old guy who died and made you wealthy. And your dad's arrest only reminds viewers you inherited your grandfather's fortune and your dad was left almost nothing. Once that's in everybody's head, the reputation you built as being one of them goes flying out the window. It's best to stay gone for another couple of months, so they don't associate you with this mess."

The reality of it washed through her. Once again, her dad had done something wrong, but she took the brunt of the punishment. "I shouldn't be penalized for something my dad did."

"And Monica Lewinsky shouldn't have spent her whole life living down one mistake. That's life in the limelight, Evie. Your name got you this job. The piece of your grandfather's charisma you were lucky enough to inherit made you a star. Now, that same name is hurting you."

She stared at him, numb but not really confused. This was what her dad did. Act without any thought for the consequences. Especially not to her.

"I think you should go back to that nice little town in Florida you've been visiting. No one found you in the months you flew back and forth from Philly. Drink some margaritas. Lay in the sun. If and when your dad's situation resolves, we'll welcome you back with open arms."

Her pride wanted to tell him that if he kicked her off the show for even two weeks, she wouldn't be back.

But she loved her show. Loved this city. She loved that she'd made something of herself after the prison of privilege she'd lived in since her mom and grandfather were killed.

She could no more tell him to shove this job than she could stop breathing. Working was her life. Having a place—a real place where people trusted her—gave meaning to what might have otherwise been a very shallow existence.

She rose slowly. "With any luck, he'll plead guilty and be out of the news cycle in a few weeks."

Marty hoisted himself from her family heirloom chair. "Exactly."

Stupid tears pooled in her eyes. She blinked them back.

Her father pleading guilty was about as farfetched as thinking he would admit that draining half her trust fund and then gambling it away had been wrong.

Marty strode to the door. "Let me suggest you get out of town before the news breaks and people start checking airline passenger lists, trying to figure out where you are. You might want to charter a private plane."

EVIE WAS STILL furious when she arrived at the Paradise Key Bed and Breakfast a little before six that evening. She'd lost the skyscraper heels, sheath, and navy jacket, replacing them with jeans, a T-shirt, boat shoes, and the biggest pair of sunglasses she owned. As if it wasn't bad enough she had to leave Philly, she'd virtually had to sneak out of town.

She carried her overnight bag across the wide front porch with white Adirondack chairs and a wooden swing, both decorated with plump orange pillows. Behind her, her cab driver hauled her two suitcases.

Taking off her sunglasses at the registration desk, she said, "Evie Barclay."

Maggie Martin's eyebrows rose, but she quickly looked away and began typing into the keyboard in front of her.

The news about her dad had broken around noon. She knew the bed and breakfast owner, just like everybody else in Paradise Key, would be aware her dad had been arrested. But no one would say anything. Paradise Key was a place to relax and lose the world, which was exactly why she was here.

Maggie handed her a key card. "It's a pleasure to have you here, Evie."

And that was the other reason she was here. The residents of Paradise Key were kind. Loyal. She might not be one of them, but she'd visited so often the past months that she was close. Like a second cousin.

"Thank you." She turned and almost ran into Lauren Webster, Jenna Davis, and Sofía Vargas. Her friends. The group she'd run with when her dad had brought her to Paradise Key to spend summers when she was a kid. She wanted to hug them, but her pride stung too much.

She fell back on her trademark sarcasm. "Shouldn't you be with your husbands?"

"Not husbands yet." Dark-haired, dark-eyed Sofía flashed her engagement ring.

Evie gaped at the beautiful diamond and laughed. "He'll be your husband soon enough."

Auburn-haired Jenna took the overnight case from Evie's hands. "Little breaks are good for relationships. Besides, we knew you'd need support."

Stunning blonde Lauren glanced around. "Where's the rest of your things?"

Evie pointed at the driver lugging her two big suitcases up the wide circular stairway. "I told him to make two trips. I know how heavy those cases are. But I think he wanted to prove he could handle them."

She sighed and looked at her friends again. "My stay is indefinite." She motioned to the stairs and Sofía, Jenna, and Lauren followed her, understanding she wouldn't want to talk in the lobby where two tourists sat pretending to read the paper as they surreptitiously cast glances her way.

Unfortunately, the only suite was on the third floor. With no elevator, it was five minutes before they got to the room, paid the taxi driver, and closed the door behind them.

Jenna faced her. "How bad is it?"

"Thirty-two counts of insider trading and all the attendant counts of things that go along with it—like fraud."

Lauren winced. "Wow."

"I was lucky one of the news department's sources got the story before it broke."

"That's shocking."

Evie sniffed a laugh. "My dad's a cheat. A thief. Nothing he does surprises me." Pain pinched her chest. She might not be surprised, but that didn't mean she couldn't be hurt. He did everything without thought for anyone but himself. Once again, he'd taken a home away from her.

She glanced around the small sitting room with a huge window overlooking the ocean. To the right was a bedroom with a four-poster bed. To the left, a wet bar. A white area rug sat on dark hardwood floors. The big window had beige trellis-print curtains that could be drawn to keep out the sun.

Obviously trying to cheer her, Lauren said, "This is lovely. I like it."

"I'm not even unpacking my suitcases. If I'm in Paradise Key indefinitely, I'm renting a beach house."

Lauren nodded.

As Jenna headed to the bedroom with the overnight bag, Sofía said, "How does your dad getting arrested force you into a leave of absence?"

"WKPP has a strict policy that on-air talent can't be the story."

Lauren frowned. "How are *you* the story?"

Evie turned away from the ocean view. "When my mom and grandfather were killed, I inherited my grandfather's fortune. My father got only my mother's estate."

Returning to the main room, Jenna said, "So? Everybody knows that."

"Lots of people also think my getting the lion's share of the money forced my dad to...steal. Or at least turn into something of a conman."

Sofía shook her head. "Nobody forces anybody else to steal."

"No, but my dad getting arrested for something that involves money puts me and my inheritance back in the news." Evie paced to the big window again. "The station manager is afraid that seeing me live again would cause a free-for-all on my life. Even without being on the air, I've had a hundred and thirty-two calls from reporters asking for a comment. Marty wasn't kidding when he said I'd need to hide out.

Which is why I'm here."

"Couldn't you tape the shows like you've been doing?"

Evie laughed. "The audience would go nuts. They could accept me taping shows while mourning the loss of a friend, but shows taped so I didn't have to answer questions about my dad would just stir everything up. Turn the situation into something it isn't." She didn't mention that if her absence lasted long enough, the audience could grow to love her replacement hosts, or the whole mess could flare up on her return. Those were things she wasn't yet ready to think about.

Sofía put her arm across Evie's shoulders. "If there's a silver lining in this, it's that you're with us."

Lauren agreed. "We can have a good time. Make it a party."

"I don't want a party. I was ready to return to work. I'm *still* ready to go back to work. What am I going to do for months that might turn into a year?"

"Sit in the sun?"

"Read?

Evie shook her head. "I've been sitting in the sun. I've been reading. You guys forget that all the weeks I've been traveling back and forth, you've had jobs. I've been bumming around. I was ready to jump back into things again. I need something to do."

Lauren brightened. "If you want to work, you could take a job with me."

"With you?" Evie's hopes built. "At the PR firm?"

"Yes, I'm in charge of the town's website, but I've gotten two new clients and need someone to take that over for me."

When Evie groaned, Laurel added, "It's already set up. Basically, all you have to do is produce the weekly video on town events for the next seven days, read the emails, update the 'happening this week' page, and make sure the live boardwalk camera is working."

The idea suddenly tempted her. Not because it was something to do, but because she would be producing a video. Not exactly a talk show, but close enough to fill a need. "I don't know."

"It's sufficient work to keep you busy and not so much to make you crazy." Lauren's voice softened. "You'd be doing me a huge favor."

Evie pulled in a breath. She did need something to do, and this sounded easy. Plus, it was more than busy work, so she wouldn't go insane or be in any of her three friends' way. It also touched on the work she loved.

The only problem was Paxton James, Paradise Key's mayor. She knew he was the star of the video...and why not? The man was gorgeous with his dark hair and green eyes. Her heart had actually stuttered when they'd been introduced at Lily's funeral. She didn't like the way she felt around him. Not weak, but silly. Goofy. Evelyn Jones Barclay did not do goofy.

Of course, working with him might be the perfect way to

discover he had feet of clay like every other man she knew. If he had a fault, making a weekly video would certainly bring it out.

Which would be the perfect way to stop all but swooning around him.

"Okay. I'll give it a try."

Her three friends sighed with relief, and Evie realized just how worried they were about her.

She batted a hand. "This will be fun."

Sofía smiled. "We'll make it fun."

Jenna said, "We all love having you here."

Lauren laughed. "Yeah, and maybe with this longer stay, we can convince you that you belong here in Paradise Key with us."

"Not on your life. I worked too hard to find a home. I'm never leaving Philly."

Evie loved her friends dearly, but it had taken her a decade to make a place for herself. She didn't want to think about how long she might be in Paradise Key or how crazy she might be driven worrying about her show, if her exile went on too long. She just prayed her dad did the right thing, pleaded guilty today, took his punishment, and let her go home again.

She internally rolled her eyes at her optimism. Still, she wouldn't let herself get down. Her dad might not plead guilty today, but if his lawyers were worth their salt, he could plead guilty sooner rather than later.

Not wanting to end the conversation on a negative note, she faced her friends. "If you guys have the night off from your men, maybe we should do dinner then find ourselves some margaritas. My treat."

They eased down the three flights of stairs, through the sedate, homespun lobby, and stepped out into the Florida sunshine, heading up the street to their favorite bar/restaurant, Scallywags.

Two feet away from the entrance, Paxton James approached them, six feet of good looks and downhome charm, not to mention a syrupy Southern accent that seriously made Evie want to swoon. Which was why she'd all but avoided him. Two failed affairs and a very bad father had taught her she and relationships didn't mix.

He nodded once as he passed them. "Ladies."

Everybody greeted him except Evie. That wonderful voice of his had made her stomach tumble.

It was stupid.

Juvenile.

And she would get past it, because she didn't want to lose the job that might preserve her sanity for the next God-only-knew-how-many months.

Chapter Two

TUESDAY MORNING, PAXTON James walked up the main street of Paradise Key, Florida, drinking in the ambiance. As a small business owner and the mayor of a town undergoing a major revitalization, his days were long. But seeing the storefronts that were being taken back to the style of Paradise Key's origin, young trees planted in boxes by parking meters, and a totally rebuilt boardwalk renewed his energy. With the renovations of the Paradise Key Resort finally begun, most of his residents would soon be gainfully employed, and business owners would be rolling in money from the small, but elite, group of tourists they hoped to attract.

If he was proud of what had been done in his years as mayor, he figured he deserved to be.

With a quick punch on the door of JavaStop, he entered the coffee shop.

"Hey, Lorelei."

The attractive owner glanced up. "Hey, Mayor! What can I get you?"

"Coffee and *this* scone," he said, pointing at the pastry inside the glass case.

She laughed. "Never met anybody so particular about his pastries."

Lorelei poured his coffee and retrieved his scone while he picked up a copy of *USA Today*. She tried to wave off his money, but he insisted on paying, then took his coffee, scone, and newspaper to one of the comfortable seats in the back.

He settled into the sand-colored traditional chair beside the matching sofa, set his coffee and scone on the glass coffee table, and opened the paper, glancing up when the door opened again.

When he saw Evelyn Barclay, he winced. She wasn't just a tall blonde drink of water; the woman was smart. The great-granddaughter of an industrialist, granddaughter of a U.S. Senator, and daughter of an activist, she'd gone to Oxford and gotten her master's at Harvard.

While she, Lauren, Jenna, and Sofía mourned the loss of their childhood friend Lily, Pax and Evie had run into each other enough that he knew to stay away from her. She was single minded. Devoted to the city of Philadelphia. And fiercely protective of her friends.

She approached his chair. "What are you doing here?"

He peered at her. Not only had she gone home a few days ago, but also her dad had gotten into big trouble the day before. He'd have thought she'd be out hiring lawyers or something.

"What are *you* doing here?"

"Looking for you."

He frowned. Oh, Lord. He could have handled the storm in her soft gray eyes, except he found it sexy. And being attracted to her was wrong for about six hundred reasons.

"Looking for me?"

"For the next few weeks, I'm in charge of the Paradise Key website. Today's the day you're supposed to be on the beach at eight." She frowned at his dress pants. "In shorts. Ready to tell people what a wonderful place Paradise Key is before rattling off this list of events." She waved a sheet like the one laying on his desk in his office in town hall.

He glanced at the list of events, and the little buzz he'd gotten staring into Evie's eyes disappeared. He hated that damned video. That was why his subconscious kept forgetting it.

"Why don't we have somebody else rattle off that list?"

She gaped at him. "You're the mayor!"

"I know...but what about you? A beautiful woman." And Lord, she was beautiful. Her blond hair hung past her shoulders in a perfect wave, her pale eyes were set in a face that could charm the angels, and her sweet voice could melt snow. Just looking at her made his head spin. "A beautiful woman with *television experience*. I'll bet you could make a much better video than I could."

"No. For a video like this, people want someone in authority."

He frowned. "How would you know?" His frown deepened. "Now that I think about it…why are you in charge of the video? Where's Lauren?"

"Working with other clients."

He sat back on the comfy sofa and crossed his arms on his chest. "Okay, I get that. But why *you?*"

"You think I can't direct a video?"

"I don't know." He rose from the sofa and took a step toward her. "This isn't exactly prime time TV. And you're behind the camera. Not in front of it. Do you have any experience? I'm not working with somebody who doesn't know what she's doing."

Her sexy eyes flashed fire again. For a few seconds, he regretted pushing her. Not just because it was a cheap excuse to get out of doing the video, but because that flash hit him right in the gut. His wife had been gone five years. Two years after her death, he'd even reentered the dating pool. But he'd never felt for any woman the weird things he felt around Evie Barclay.

What was he doing egging her on?

"Look, just tell Lauren I'm not doing the video anymore." He returned to his seat and picked up the paper, mindlessly opening it. He couldn't get the strange tingling sensation out of his chest, and if her eyes were still flashing fire, he didn't want to see it.

"You're doing the video."

He turned a page in the paper. "No. I'm not."

"Oh, yeah. You are."

Her voice sounded so positive, so sure, that he let the paper crumble. "You come up to my shoulder, and I don't think you weigh a hundred and twenty pounds. You don't scare me."

"Yeah, well, what if we have Tyson Braddock do it? The guy who wants your job." She laughed. "This is sort of a backhanded way of giving it to him."

Her mention of his rival made him laugh. "You know what? We asked him. Even *he* doesn't want to do it."

She groaned. "Come on! It's one stupid video. Once a week. All you have to do is read a list."

"And look like a piece of cardboard with permanently bugged eyes. Some of us were not made for the camera." But she was. Her hair was glorious. Her eyes were tantalizing. Her smile made him want to sigh. She was perfect. "I still think you should do it. Come on. Please? I'd try to bribe you, but I know you don't need money."

"No. I don't." Her anger faded, and she stepped back. "But even if I did, I'm staying out of the limelight for a few weeks."

Remorse filled him. Of all the stupid things to say, nagging her to do the video was the stupidest. Yesterday, it had been only a matter of hours before people added her father's arrest with her sudden reappearance in his secluded small town and realized she was hiding out. Her dad was a criminal. She'd been gossiped about her entire life. She'd lost her mom the way his daughter Samantha had lost hers. She was the poster child for the saying *money does not buy happiness.*

And suddenly, all his good arguments about not doing the video sounded like mean-spirited tantrums in his head.

With a heavy sigh, he folded the paper. "All right. I'll do this week's video, but then I want you guys to come up with another plan." He paused, cutting her a look. "I mean it."

She shrugged. "I'm not management. I'm just the hired help. If you want to change the plan, you have to talk to Lauren."

He wondered if he hadn't been hornswoggled. Or if his own dumb soft heart had read things into the situation that weren't there. He'd seen her on the beach reading, seen her in Scallywags enjoying her friends. If she was staying out of the limelight, it wasn't because she was hurt. It was because she didn't want to damage the pristine reputation she had in Philly.

Still, he *was* kind of stuck. He pointed at the door. "Let's go."

He didn't know why she was helping Lauren, but after the way Evie had conned him, he suspected it involved something for Evie. He'd learned that from his television star mom. Ten years in one of TV's most popular sitcoms had netted her a bundle, but she'd spent it all trying to develop another show for herself. When that didn't work, she'd borrowed money, trying to create shows for him and his younger sister. She'd dragged them to development meetings, sent them to dance classes and singing lessons—not to mention class after class of acting techniques—made them run lines in front of producers and directors, and in general stolen their childhoods…while wasting a fortune. Not because she wanted them to be happy, but because she wanted the fame back. Jenny James did nothing that didn't benefit her.

Evie Barclay might not want the limelight, but she wanted something.

He opened the JavaStop door and let Evie out first. "I'll go home and change, then meet you on the boardwalk."

Evie nodded and started down the street, but he stopped her. "And, Evie? We run through this once and only once. So get it on the first take."

He turned and headed in the other direction. It was a small demand, but it somehow made him feel the tiniest bit better. How could her attractiveness have made him forget for even one second that some people only looked out for themselves?

He hurried down the street, across two blocks and down another to his house, a blue-shingled Victorian with a wide porch that fronted the entire structure and wrapped around the left side. White columns ran from roof to floor, matching the spindle railing that gave it a cozy, homey feel. He strode up to the double front doors, black with etched glass cut in sections, held together in black iron frames that gave them an art-deco feel.

Opening the door, he called, "Samantha?"

He'd left the Victorian style behind when he remodeled the inside. Touches like the fireplace, crown molding, and original hardwood floors—which he refinished a stunning gray—remained. But the open-floorplan displayed a bright white kitchen, dining area with white tufted chairs around a reclaimed wood table, and a living room with a flat-screen TV that served as a mirror when it wasn't displaying shows.

His twelve-year-old daughter came flying down the stairs. Her dark hair wasn't caught up in the usual ponytail. Instead, it hung past her shoulders, poker straight and shining, as if it had just been washed. Her wide brown eyes, so much like her mother's, sat in a face made up of high cheekbones and a straight nose, with peaches-and-cream skin.

As she'd grown taller, she'd also begun losing baby fat. Today, she wore scruffy jeans with a dressy blue blouse with bell sleeves. He'd thought a T-shirt would look better with the jeans, or dress pants with the pretty blouse, but when he'd mentioned it, Samantha had laughed.

"What do you want?"

"I'm changing clothes, and then I need you to come with me to make the video for the town website."

Her eyes widened. "You want me to be in the video?"

He sighed. If only she could...

"No. I want you to come along. I don't want you to be alone. You can't spend all day, every day in the house. It's not right." It wasn't really a lie. Since summer vacation started, he'd been worried about her. In the evenings, she'd been quiet and moody, staying in her room when she normally came downstairs to watch TV with him. He couldn't take her to the office. Too boring. But she could accompany him to the boardwalk and hang out while Evie and her crew set up.

And if Samantha also kept him too busy to interact with Evie, that was just a bonus.

IT DIDN'T TAKE a lot to set up for a video to be put on a website. A sixth grader with a phone could have done it. In fact, the technician hired by Lauren's firm had told Evie it would probably be easier to use a phone.

Pax didn't show up for twenty minutes. Evie had only needed five to get back to the boardwalk, so she and Dave had been waiting for fifteen boring minutes. She swiped the hair from her face, but the breeze off the gulf blew it back again.

"How can it take twenty minutes for a guy to remove one shirt and one pair of pants and replace them?"

Dave Calhoun laughed. "Maybe he's having trouble figuring out what to wear?"

Even as he said that, Evie saw the mayor of Paradise Key coming around the side of the resort. He wore board shorts and a big T-shirt, exactly what they wanted for the video.

A few quick strides took him past the scaffolding and construction workers and onto the boardwalk—

With his daughter.

Everything inside Evie stewed. She had the oddest sense he was going to say he couldn't tape today because he had to babysit.

It was ridiculous. But he was being ridiculous.

In this day and age of casual videos, who argued about rattling off a list on camera?

She and Dave headed over to meet them. "Mr. Mayor." She smiled at Samantha. "I see you brought your daughter."

"I thought she might enjoy watching us make the video."

Okay. Evie could accept that. She could even counteract it. "That's great. Samantha, do you want to stand behind Dave with me?"

Her already big eyes widened. "You mean like a director?"

"Sure! Why not?"

Dave hit a few buttons on his unnecessarily advanced camera. "Ready?"

Paxton said, "Ready," and ambled farther down the boardwalk, so the video wouldn't pick up the renovations on the resort, but would get the ocean and incredibly blue sky as the backdrop. A few beachgoers were already setting up. The wind had enticed out a couple with a kite. The air smelled like heaven as the surf rolled toward the shore.

It was perfect.

Dave raised his hand, counting down from five with his fingers. "Five, four, three, two, one..." He pointed at Paxton.

"Hey! It's a glorious eighty-one degrees here in Paradise Key, Florida." Pax held out his hands as if embracing the warmth. Then he started moving toward the camera, just as they'd done in the videos they'd already made.

"This week, there's a chili cookoff sponsored by the ladies' auxiliary to benefit the fire company." He motioned down the boardwalk. "Stroll up and down all day and sample the offerings. At the end of the day, pick your favorite and make somebody's day."

Evie sighed. "Cut!"

Pax stopped dead. Dave turned to look at her.

She shook her head. "It's a little thing, but saying at the end of the day, make somebody's day... It's repetitive. Especially after you'd already said stroll up and down all day."

Pax crossed his arms on his chest. "We said one take."

She laughed, but when he just stared at her, she said, "I thought you were kidding."

"I wasn't."

"No one does these things in one take."

Samantha solemnly said, "It's true, Dad. Some of my friends tweak their YouTube videos for hours."

"There! See," Evie said, suddenly glad he'd brought his

daughter. "Even people who post pictures of their dogs do more than one take."

"My friends don't post dogs." Samantha glanced at her dad, and then back to Evie. "They post makeup tips."

"Oh. I did show on that in Philly."

Samantha's eyes brightened. "You did?"

"Yes. Those videos are very popular. One of the best ways to keep up with makeup trends."

"Hello," Pax called, waving his hands. "Mayor needs to get back to work."

"Oh, right!" Evie turned to Samantha. "When your dad leaves, you and I can get a coffee, then I'll tell you the top three videos I found."

"Great."

Dave threw her a patient look.

"Oh! Sorry again." She motioned to Dave. "Start when you're ready."

Pax backed up. Dave hit a few buttons on the camera. "Five, four, three, two, one..." He pointed at Paxton.

"Hey! It's a glorious eighty-one degrees here today in Paradise Key, Florida." Pax held out his hands as if embracing the warmth, then started moving toward the camera.

"This week, there's a chili cookoff sponsored by the ladies' auxiliary to benefit the fire company." He motioned down the boardwalk. "Stroll along all day and sample the offerings. When you're done, pick your favorite. See how your taste stacks up against everyone else's."

"Cut!"

Everybody glanced at Samantha. "Dad, the wind's making a mess of your hair."

"My hair is supposed to look windblown," Pax said in exasperation. "I'm at the beach. We're trying to give people the full experience."

She pulled a comb from her pocket. "You look like Einstein. Last week, my friends did memes."

"Memes? What the hell's a meme?"

Dave leaned toward Pax. "It's where people create cartoons to make fun of something."

He gaped at his daughter. "People made fun of me?"

"Only your hair." She handed him the comb.

He took it, ran it through his hair, and handed it back. "Can we do this all ready?"

"Sure," Evie said, stifling a laugh.

"I see that smirk."

"I was just thinking that somebody in the public eye as much as you are should be accustomed to criticism."

"Of my policies? Yes. Of my hair?" He shook his head. "That's just stupid."

Dave mumbled. "That's the digital age."

Evie took a breath to stop a laugh that spilled out and composed herself the way she did before the cameras were turned on her every day at noon. "Count it down, Dave."

He did the countdown, and they started from the top. It took three more tries before they finally got it right.

Chapter Three

ANNOYED IT HAD taken so long, Pax approached Evie. "Lauren never did more than three takes."

"I did what I had to do to get a good video."

Samantha sighed. "Dad, two of the cuts were mine."

Was she defending Evie? He shook his head in dismay. The memory of being a kid in a sitcom washed over him. Fifteen takes for something as simple as licking an ice cream cone wasn't merely tiring; it had been embarrassing with his mom constantly calling cut, trying to show off for the director. But he didn't like to remember those days. And he certainly wouldn't talk about them. He was over all that. He ambled back to his office, leaving Samantha in Evie's hands because Evie had promised to take her to the coffee shop.

He entered the Paxton Properties office, where he sometimes worked mornings. His secretary, forty-year-old Dotty Barnes, handed him his messages.

Scampering behind him as he strode into his office, she unnecessarily told him their contents. "You've had two calls from Tyler. I think he wants to butter you up, so you'll vote his way on that taffy sign policy. There's a call from a trash hauler. I think he's trying to make inroads on your rental properties. And two calls from reporters wanting to know about the resort renovations."

"Forward those to Lauren Walker."

But thinking about Lauren reminded him of Evie. Multiple takes of a stupid video, cozying up to his daughter…having coffee with her right now—

He paused. His precious daughter, who didn't need her head filled with all kinds of crazy thoughts from a rich woman slumming in their small town, was having coffee with Evie?

Oh Lord! He'd been so flummoxed by the takes he'd left his daughter with a woman so wealthy and casually famous she probably had no idea what happened in the real world.

He turned back to the door. "I need another twenty minutes, Dotty."

He sped out of his office and raced up Second Street on his way to JavaStop. But he saw Evie a few yards ahead of him.

Confusion poured through him. She'd abandoned Samantha? She'd taken Sam to JavaStop and left her?

He quickened his steps until he caught up to her. "Where's Sam?"

She glanced over, furrowing her brow. "At home. She said she didn't want coffee, and it was too hot for cocoa. We talked about the makeup videos as I walked her home, and then we said goodbye." Her eyes narrowed. "Why? You thought I'd dumped her?"

He raised his hands. "I didn't know what to think."

She studied his face, then sighed. "It doesn't matter. I didn't leave her. I made sure she got home. She's a great kid, by the way."

Pax had never felt stupider. He'd made a lot of mistakes in his life. Some bigger than others. But for some reason or another, thinking Evie had dumped Sam filled him with a combination of embarrassment and humiliation that was nearly intolerable.

"She *is* a great kid."

Evie bumped his shoulder with her own. "Having a little trouble being nice to me, aren't you?"

He almost told her he was having trouble with her period. Forget about being nice. Being so wrong about her was excruciating because she *was* damned close to perfect. She was pretty, smart, and sort of funny.

During her initial visits, he could see her from a far, acknowledge she was attractive, and forget her. Working with her and having her make friends with his daughter put her in his life. He couldn't think about her being pretty and scramble away. He had to admit she was way out of his league and deal with her. Deal with things like the question she'd just asked.

"You don't exactly love me, either."

She shrugged. "I have a bad history with men."

He laughed. Like he believed a gorgeous blonde with money was a man repellant.

"I do! My dad sent me to boarding school, barely talked to me when I was home, and used my trust fund like a bank. I give the first guy who broke my heart a pass because everybody gets their heart broken by their first love. But the next two guys were just jerks."

"You do know you have to take some credit for some of that, right?"

She gaped at him.

"You picked the two jerks."

She laughed, and the embarrassed/humiliated feeling about killing Paxton lessened. Okay. So she wasn't perfect. She was human. She'd been hurt.

In a way, that made things worse. That meant he had no reason to scurry off. Soon, she was going to realize just how attracted he was to her, and she'd probably tease the hell out of him.

When they reached Pete's Newsstand, she stopped and grabbed a copy of the *Paradise Key Gazette*.

"Looking for some heavy reading?"

She shook her head. "I might as well catch up on things. I don't know how long I'm going to be here." She caught his gaze. "I'm hiding out."

"Yeah, you mentioned that." And he felt like crap again. The woman was rich, pampered. How could she look so world-weary and vulnerable?

The embarrassed/humiliated feeling morphed into empathy. Instead of thinking she was like his mom, he suddenly wondered if her dad hadn't treated her a lot like how his mom had treated him.

"Anyway, since I'll be here a while, I was thinking about renting a beach house. Somewhere I could get comfortable, spread out, have friends over."

His conscience tweaked. He had several rental properties. One he'd just finished a remodel on, so it was open for the entire year. He could rent it to her. Except—

Now that they were talking like normal people, he didn't feel tongue-tied around her. He had a serious case of the warm fuzzies. He was attracted to her. Any man worth his salt would be. And now he was beginning to like her? That was a recipe for disaster.

"A beach house would be nice."

"You're the mayor. You probably know every property in town. Any suggestions?"

There went his conscience again. He did know every property in town. He *had* a property she could rent. She was a nice woman, just trying to protect herself the way he had been guarding himself his entire life. And here he was, thinking about himself.

He squeezed his eyes shut, drew in a breath, and then opened them. "There is a place that doesn't have any bookings all summer."

"How do you know?"

"I own it."

"You own it?" She swatted him with the newspaper.

"And you let me stand here and all but grovel for help?"

"You might not like the house."

"Beggars can't be choosers." She stopped, angling toward him. "Where is it?"

"A bit down the beach." He paused and decided he might as well plunge in. "In the mood for a walk?"

She glanced at her boat shoes. "I think so."

EVIE AND PAX strolled down the long stretch of white sand drenched in hot summer sun. A small strip of hotels and bed and breakfasts gave way to a bit of undeveloped land, then one-story houses began to pop up, old-style, well-kept havens with the feeling of home.

Evie gasped. Pax hadn't had to say a word when they got close to the one he had available to rent. The little aqua ranch with white shutters had a huge back deck and art-deco doors, similar to the ones on the Victorian he'd remodeled for himself. Evie had seen them when she'd escorted Samantha home.

She faced him with a grin, stifling the urge to hug him. "I love it."

"You haven't seen the inside."

Okay, she and Pax had never been BFFs, but she'd thought they were beginning to get along. Why didn't he want to rent to her?

They made their way to the porch in silence, except for the rattle of keys as Pax located the one for the deck doors.

As he inserted it into the lock, she said, "You never did answer my question about not liking me."

"It's not a matter of liking. It's a matter of trusting."

That was a weird thing to say. "You can't mistrust me. You don't know me."

"And we were getting along very well not knowing each other."

She frowned. That didn't make any sense either. "What you're telling me is you don't like being around me?"

"I didn't say that."

He had. Just not directly. After Lily's accident, Evie had gotten a crush on him, and he'd been avoiding her?

Actually, she'd been avoiding him too. Because she was attracted to him. Physically. What if he—

She almost laughed.

He didn't like her. But he could very possibly be attracted to her.

He opened the door on a great room that could only be described as a show piece. A white fireplace dominated the space, accenting dark hardwood floors. Airy light filled the white kitchen, easily seen in the open-floor plan. Fat yellow, brown, and blue pillows sat on angled chairs and sofas, making them soft and comfortable looking.

"Holy cow."

"What? Didn't expect to find something like this in a

small town?"

"I don't know what I expected. But you're not going to make me feel like I look down on you or this town. I might have money, but I behave like a normal person."

"Of course you do." He motioned for her to enter the house. "Let's go inside."

"You're not going to pretend to agree with me to dodge this discussion. If I'm going to rent from you and live in your town—maybe for a year while my dad does a song and dance trying to convince the SEC he's an innocent victim—I think we should get along."

"There's no reason for us to get along." He pointed down a small hall. "There are two bedrooms back there."

"Why is there no reason for us to get along?" She was pushing. Wanting him to admit he was attracted to her. Mostly for a laugh. She'd fought the same odd feeling around him, so hearing him admit his attraction would be fun.

Or...

Maybe instead of fighting it, they should enjoy it. He was single and gorgeous. She was single and stuck in this town. Maybe a fling could brighten both of their days a bit.

He pivoted and started in the other direction. "And down here is the master." He opened the door on an amazing room with double glass doors that displayed a breathtaking view of the ocean. A California king sat on a taupe area rug that covered a portion of the dark hardwood floors. Open barn doors displayed a bathroom with a clawfoot tub, a shower big enough for the cast of *Game of Thrones*, and a black vanity with double sinks and white baskets for linens.

All thought of their attraction forgotten, she sighed. "Who does your decorating?"

"I pick things I think other people will like."

She glanced around in awe. "You are very good."

He cleared his throat. "My wife taught me."

"Oh." Suddenly, instinctively, she understood why he was so standoffish. Why he'd never have something as mundane as a fling. Everybody knew his wife had died. Everybody liked and pampered his motherless daughter. But Evie had never thought of his wife as a person until this very second. A person Pax hadn't just loved, but who'd shared his life, his visions.

And he didn't want to be attracted to another woman.

Or maybe he didn't want to be attracted to a woman so different from his wife?

Bingo. Not only did that explanation seem right, but also it made her settle down and stop teasing him.

She could almost feel his late wife's presence—at the very least see her influence. Evie stepped back, awkward and tongue-tied for the first time since she'd stopped making excuses for her dad.

"Well…" The word tiptoed into the difficult silence. "It's perfect, and I'd like to rent it." She carefully turned to catch his gaze. His solemn green eyes held hers. "I'm sure you have a lease form lying around somewhere."

"In my office."

"Great. Want to go back and get it?"

He motioned to the door. "No." He took the key off the ring and handed it to her. "You can move in this afternoon if you want. Stop at my office tomorrow morning. I'll have a lease ready then."

With that, he abruptly strode out the back door, across the deck, and into the sand.

Evie watched him go. She was a bit sorry she'd teased him, but a lot sorrier she wouldn't get the chance to tease him again.

She'd had fun with him, but he didn't seem to want to enjoy himself. It was as sad as it was blissfully romantic. She couldn't imagine any of her boyfriends or lovers ever being so distraught by losing her that they wouldn't want another woman even five years after she was gone.

THE NEXT MORNING, Jenna jerked her SUV to a stop in front of Evie's newly rented beach house.

"Oh, it's lovely," Lauren exclaimed.

Sofía agreed. "Pax does amazing work."

Evie opened her door and jumped out. "How is it every-body knew he restored beach houses except me?"

Lauren joined her on the short driveway. "Because he doesn't merely restore beach houses. He manages properties. He buys things, and then fixes them up to rent or flip." She shrugged. "Or just hold onto until the market is better."

Sofía also climbed out of the SUV. "Some of which just happen to be beach houses."

Evie grabbed her heaviest bag, leaving the second case for Sofía and Jenna to fight over. When they reached the front door—another art-deco masterpiece that matched the one on the back deck—she tossed the keys to Lauren.

When the door opened, all three of Evie's friends gasped. "Oh, he's outdone himself this time."

Evie rolled her big suitcase down the hall to the master with Jenna on her heels. Sofía and Lauren followed.

"Can we help you unpack?"

Evie hoisted the case onto the bed. "Sure. I'll unpack, and you guys can watch."

Jenna tossed the second case on the bed and opened it to reveal jeans, shorts, and tops. A couple of pairs of flip-flops were tucked in the side pockets. "I can do these." She pointed at a dresser. "Most of it should go in those drawers anyway."

"Okay."

Being in the gorgeous master had Evie thinking about Pax's wife again. About Pax being in love with someone, and his sweet daughter missing her mother. All three of her friends would have known the woman who inspired such loyalty.

She bit her bottom lip, trying to keep herself from asking the obvious. In the end, though, her curiosity won. "He told me his wife taught him to decorate."

"She had a good eye," Sofía said.

"Fabulous dresser," Jenna agreed.

"Was she nice?"

Jenna stopped halfway to the dresser. Sofía's eyebrows rose. Lauren laughed. "I think somebody has a crush on our mayor."

"This isn't about a crush. This is about him. All yesterday, I sensed something odd with him. It took me hours before I realized he was attracted to me. Then I started goofing around—I guess I wanted to get him to admit it. But when he told me about his wife, everything fizzled."

A stack of jeans in one hand, Jenna tugged a drawer open with the other. "Some people say he's not over her."

"Oh." It was one thing to think of teasing and having fun with a regular guy. But Pax wasn't a regular guy. He was a widower. Someone who'd had his heart shattered by loss.

Sofía sat on the bed near the suitcase Evie had yet to open. "She was very special."

"Pretty?"

Lauren laughed. "Gorgeous. Just look at Samantha, imagine her as an adult, and you have Elizabeth."

"Elizabeth?" Evie turned the name over on her tongue, telling herself she was only curious because in the oddest way, she felt like she was living with the woman. Or at the very least living with her taste in home furnishing.

"Anyway," Jenna continued. "She's been gone a few years now. I'll bet he's ready for a juicy affair."

Evie laughed. "I was on the verge of thinking that yesterday until he brought me here. He seemed sad. Lost. I don't want to mess with that."

Sofía groaned. "Oh, but it could be so good for him!"

Lauren sidled up to Evie and peeked over her shoulder. "And you."

"It could also end horribly and ruin the rest of my stay here."

Jenna had finished unpacking her bag, but Evie hadn't even started the one she'd carted to the bed. "You know what? You guys have jobs to get to, and I should be at Pax's office in a few minutes to sign the lease."

Lauren grinned. "Can we come?"

"No!" Evie shook her head. "I'm serious. Number one, I'm unhappy enough considering I'm on leave from a job I miss. I don't want to make things worse by messing around with the mayor and starting gossip. Number two, the man looked miserable when he was showing me the place. Let's leave him alone."

That explanation satisfied her friends. They all piled back into Jenna's SUV. After dropping her off on the sidewalk in front of Paxton Properties, they waved and headed off again. Evie sucked in a breath, straightened her sky-blue T-shirt over her jeans, and marched to the door.

She opened it to find a red-haired receptionist.

"Can I help you?" the woman politely asked.

"I rented Pax's…the mayor's…um, Mr. James' beach house yesterday."

"Oh, that's right. You must be Evie?"

She wasn't surprised the receptionist knew her name. After her father's national-news arrest and yesterday's resultant gossip, the entire planet knew her name.

"He told me you'd taken the old Golden place." The woman stood and offered her hand. "I'm Dotty."

Evie shook it. "Nice to meet you."

Dotty turned and called, "Hey, Pax, Evie's here to sign her lease."

Evie winced.

"I heard you talking to her, Dotty. Give me two seconds to pull it from the pile."

Dotty leaned across the desk. "Just go ahead on in."

Evie held back a laugh. "Thanks."

Trying to appear nonchalant, she ambled to the open door of Pax's office and tapped on the doorframe. "Hey."

He didn't even look up. "Hey." He shuffled some papers. "Here it is. I had Dotty fill in the particulars and print it this morning, but then the mail came and buried it."

She smiled and gingerly moved toward his desk. "It's good you found it."

He nodded. "Have a seat."

She sat on the chair across from his desk, leaning forward when he slid a copy of the lease over to her. She read the two pages in about a minute and a half. It was a standard lease— no funny business or signing away her firstborn child.

"Looks good."

"It's standard."

"I can see that."

She liked it much better when they were angry with or teasing one another. This new normal dripped with tension.

He handed her a pen. She signed the lease, scooting it back for him to add his signature. Dotty meandered in, taking the contract to make a copy. She folded it and put into an envelope, which Evie slid it into her purse. With no fanfare, everybody proceeded to the office door. Apparently in the South, nobody saw themselves out.

When they were two feet away from the door, it opened. The bell tinkled as sunlight poured in, momentarily blinding Evie, preventing her from seeing the person who'd entered.

She stepped back, Pax and Dotty mirroring her movement. The door closed. And suddenly, there he was...

Her father.

Chapter Four

"WHAT ARE YOU *doing* here?"

Paxton stood in the center of the reception area of his small office, feeling the way a person probably feels when he sees a tornado roaring toward him.

"I asked the cabbie where to rent a private, secluded beach house, and he brought me here." Evie's dad, a tall, dark-haired gentleman dressed in charcoal-gray trousers, a white shirt, and navy-blue blazer, gaped at his daughter. "What are you doing here?"

"I am hiding out from the press because of you!"

"And you were doing it so well, I decided I should join you. But I wasn't talking about Paradise Key. I was talking about this rental office. You're staying at the bed and breakfast. I had hoped to get something far away from you, so you wouldn't know I was here."

Pax could see Evie shaking, but he couldn't tell if it was with rage or confusion. He faced her dad. "You want a beach house?"

The man nodded.

"One bedroom? Two?"

"I'd like two. I have a friend who might visit."

Evie's mouth fell open. "You're bringing friends? I might as well pack and go now. In two days, this place will be crawling with reporters."

"Calm down."

Her dad's voice was deep, solemn. The kind one usually heard in television commercials. Which shouldn't have surprised Pax. Everybody knew her dad had been a successful actor when he married Evie's socialite mom.

"I covered my tracks. And my attorney knows where I am. There'll be no manhunt or Feds storming the town."

Pax stepped to a board of keys on the wall. He plucked off a set and tossed them to his receptionist. "Dotty, why don't you show Mr. Barclay the Evan's house?"

Dotty gasped. "Oh, that one's lovely." She grabbed her purse from her drawer and walked around her desk. Getting between Evie and her dad. Catching Finn Barclay's arm, she turned him toward the exit. "You will love this house!"

Opening the door, she ushered him out. "Two gorgeous bedrooms and a deck that's to die for. Of course, we provide a grill. And linens—"

Dotty's voice trailed away as the door closed behind them.

Paxton surveyed Evie. "You okay?"

"That stupid old man."

Finn hadn't looked a day over fifty to Pax, though given Evie's age of thirty, he was probably closer to sixty. But there was no way anybody could call Finn Barclay an old man.

"Okay. I get that you don't like him, but it's not a good idea to say bad things about your father. You know. Karma and all that."

"He just can't let me alone."

"It sounded like he has every intention of leaving you alone."

Evie paced to the coat tree and back again. "Oh, sure. That's what he says. But this time tomorrow, he'll be at my door borrowing a cup of sugar."

"Don't tell him which beach house you're staying in."

She snorted. "He'll find it."

Pax sighed. She was right. Paradise Key wasn't big enough to keep that secret. "Yeah. He probably will." He took in her hair, now disheveled from the way she'd plowed her fingers through it, and the sadness in her eyes. "I'm sorry."

She sucked in a breath. "I am, too. I was really looking forward to a nice stay." She shot a grin at him. "I was even going to flirt with you. Maybe turn that flirting into an affair."

His stomach took a tumble. No woman had ever spoken to him so boldly. He decided her bravado was an attempt to push past her upset over her dad, and he tried to make a joke. "Well, fun as that sounds, that isn't why I was sorry. I'm sorry because your lease is binding. You're stuck here."

THAT STUPIDITY OF what he said popped Evie's anger like a bubble, and she burst out laughing.

"That's better."

How one simple comment could hold so much warmth and intimacy, Evie didn't know, but the fact that he cared enough to make her laugh drifted through her like an unexpected breeze. Then she noticed how close they were, and something fizzed in her stomach. Anticipation? No. That wasn't quite it. This was different, felt different.

She didn't know what the hell it was. Having her dad arrive had thrown her so far off balance she might never right herself.

She shook her head to clear it of that thought. Evie Barclay never lost control. Not with her dad. And not with the very sexy mayor. The simple thing to do would be avoid them both.

She took a step back. "You know I could buy my way out of that lease."

"You could. Or I could tear it up." Totally ruining her plan to avoid him, he turned her to face him and put his hands on her shoulders.

Tingles of something she could neither define nor describe raced through her. They worsened when she caught the gaze of his gorgeous green eyes.

"But, Evie, tearing up your lease isn't the thing to do. First, you already ran once. From Philly to here. You don't want to run again. Second, your support system is here.

Third, I don't think your dad's going to bother you."

"Of course he is. Pretending he's mad at me, that he didn't want me to know he's here…that's an act."

"Aren't you going a little overboard?"

"You don't know my dad."

He removed his hands from her shoulders. "You're right. I don't." He inhaled and added, "The ink is barely dry on the lease. I'll give you three days to think it through." He regarded her seriously. "Just don't do anything rash."

With a quick nod of agreement, Evie stepped out into the hot Florida sun. She looked left, then right, and groaned. This would be what she'd be doing every time she went outside, entered a restaurant, went for coffee, or walked into a shop: searching for her dad.

Fury raced through her. She'd spent ten years avoiding him, living on her own, *enjoying* her life. Why did he have to invade her space? She snorted. More important? Why did he have to cheat, lie, and steal? Why couldn't he have been a normal dad?

PAX WATCHED EVIE leave, tracking her progress until she ducked into JavaStop. He'd never met anyone as alone as she was. Not that she didn't have friends. She had three great ones here in Paradise Key and undoubtedly many others in Philly. But a man didn't have to be a shrink to realize she held something of herself back.

He shook his head as he ducked into his office. He wasn't Dr. Phil, and he didn't want to care about Evie Barclay. He had a town renovation that was just barely on target, a daughter entering puberty, and a celebrity viewing another of his properties with Dotty.

As mayor, he had to be concerned about the media finding Finn Barclay.

As a dad, he was unprepared for what his daughter's teen years might bring.

And back to being mayor, he also had to be concerned that the bad blood between Evie and her dad might come to a showdown. In his small town.

That would make national news.

There were too many people who could take a video with their phones. These days, there were too many people who'd see the money from the major networks, get stars in their eyes, and happily sell their footage.

He shouldn't have talked Evie into staying. He should have let her go.

Except she belonged here. Her dad didn't. Evie had friends here. She should stay. Finn Barclay should go.

Sitting behind his desk, he went to work, writing up a contract to buy an apartment building that he planned to turn into condos. Twenty minutes later, he heard the tinkle of the bell above his door and watched Dotty and Finn enter, laughing.

"What a great story!"

"I have a million of them. I cherished my time with the Kennedys in Hyannis Port and the Bushes at Kennebunkport."

Dotty wave a hand. "To heck with politicians. I love the stories about the movie stars."

Finn made a gesture that ended with him pointing at Dotty. "Maybe you and I should have dinner tonight."

Dotty's eyes widened. "I would love that. Howard, my husband, would enjoy meeting you."

Even from his desk, Pax could see the disappointment flit across Finn's face.

"Your husband?"

"Oh, I'm sorry. I didn't think to tell you." She glanced down at her hand and gasped. "I forgot! My ring is at the jeweler."

Pax decided this was the perfect moment to interrupt. He pushed back his chair, rising to stride into the reception area.

"Mr. Barclay," he said, motioning him forward. "Why don't you come into my office?"

Finn loosened his shoulders. "I think I'll get going. I already signed the lease."

Pax's face fell. "You did?"

Dotty smiled, obviously pleased with herself. "I always keep one in my purse."

"That's great," Pax said. "But there are a few things Mr.

Barclay and I need to go over."

"Like what?" Dotty's chipper tone turned defensive. "I know the drill."

"Yes. You're a champ," Pax agreed. He approached Finn and put his hand on his shoulder to direct him into the office. As soon as Finn cleared the door, Pax closed it. No need for Dotty to overhear this and print a newsletter for her friends.

"Have a seat."

Finn sat as Pax returned to his chair behind his desk.

"Nice place you have here."

His office wasn't anything to brag about. The decorating details he'd picked up from his late wife hadn't extended to this space. He loved that his home was beautiful for Samantha. He appreciated that his properties were beautiful for his renters. But this barebones, masculine area with a picture of a shipwreck on the far wall and a coat tree from the eighteen hundreds was all his. A place he could think. One that mirrored the emptiness he always felt.

"I like to think of it as austere."

Finn tossed him a smile. "It's certainly that. So, what is it you want? You can't care that I've been arrested. You knew that before you sent Dotty and me out to look at the place." He paused, his thick black brows drooping together. "You sweet on my daughter, boy?"

Finn's deep, rumbling voice mixed with the angry expression on his movie-star face almost sent Pax into cardiac arrest.

"No!" It wasn't precisely a lie. He might find Evie Barclay incredibly attractive, but sweet did not describe what he felt for her.

Pax sat forward and folded his hands on the desk, atop the reams of paper Tyson Braddock had needed to write a new ordinance. "I was just thinking that perhaps your being here might not be a good idea."

"You *are* sweet on her."

"I'm not sweet on her," Pax insisted. "Good God, the woman's like a barracuda sometimes."

Finn laughed. "Gets that from her mother."

Remembering Finn had lost his wife, the same way Pax had lost Elizabeth, nudged his empathy button.

"I'm sorry for your loss," he said quietly.

"It was a long time ago. But Dotty tells me you lost your wife more recently."

"It's been five years." He still remembered the night. Unexpectedly cold in Florida and so dark the streetlights barely lit the way to the ambulance. Pain filled his chest as the memories flooded his brain. The race to the hospital. The doctor telling him Elizabeth was gone.

He shook his head to clear it. "But to get back to Evie, she's got friends here. Good ones who can help her through getting put on administrative leave."

Finn's head snapped up. "She was put on administrative leave? What did she do? Defend me?"

Pax stared at him for a few seconds. For such a cultured, good-looking guy, Finn Barclay was incredibly clueless. "She was put on administrative leave *because of* you. I don't know much about television, but I found a few older versions of Evie's show on YouTube. Fans call in and ask her questions. I'm sure her bosses didn't want people phoning in to ask about you." He paused and caught Finn's gaze. "Your situation."

"You looked up my daughter on YouTube? Are you some kind of stalker, boy?"

"No! Evie was here all spring with her friends." Pax sat up a little straighter in his chair. "I'm mayor of this town. Evie's a celebrity. I had to make sure she wasn't going to do something like bring her cameramen down and produce a show here."

"That's a very weak argument."

A little tired of this guy's condescension, Pax looked him right in the eye. "I have a town to run. A town to protect. I don't take that lightly." He almost added he also didn't take raising his daughter lightly, but he didn't play dirty. Evie's troubles with her dad were her business. "Back then, I was making sure we weren't caught with our pants down. Today, I'm warning you upfront that I won't tolerate a scene. If even one reporter shows up, that lease you signed will get torn up so fast your head will spin."

"I'll fight it."

"I'll let you. I'll give you back every cent of money

you've paid without blinking an eye because the sanctity and safety of my town is what matters to me."

Finn sniffed, rising stiffly from his chair. "I have no intention of bringing reporters here. I'm hiding as much as Evie is."

"Then stay away from her."

Finn smiled thinly. "Oh, now, son, that you can't dictate."

"Whatever you think you want from her, you're not going to get it."

Finn laughed. "Really? You have a daughter, right?"

Pax said nothing.

"Ten years is a hell of a long time not to talk. Now, I'm facing a decade in prison. Add that ten years to the first ten of not talking and I'm afraid we'll never speak again." He buttoned his navy blazer and turned to the door, but spun around again. "And believe it or not, I'm not doing this for me. I'm doing it for Evie." He held Pax's gaze. "Think about your own daughter. About how your wife would feel if you left her alone her entire life."

With that, he strode out of Pax's office.

After he heard the outer door slam, Pax got up to lean against his doorframe.

Dotty quietly said, "I guess this means I don't get dinner."

"Neither does Howard."

Dotty chuckled. "Yeah. Big mistake not wearing a ring."

She brightened. "But it's awful nice to have a former movie star think I'm attractive enough to have dinner with."

Pax shook his head. "This isn't funny. Evie hates him. He hurt her. And now he's going to try to win her back in our town."

"Maybe we shouldn't be so worried about the town?"

Pax frowned. "We should be worried about him?"

"No. We should be worried about Evie. What if he isn't lying? What if he's really doing this for her?"

Pax snorted.

"Then answer his other question. What would Elizabeth think if you left Samantha alone and didn't talk to her for ten years?"

Thinking of Elizabeth brought incredible pain. She'd been beautiful, smart, charismatic. But not in the way Evie was. Liz was the kind of woman who brought soup in a crisis, while Evie was the kind who would bring the community together in a crisis.

He shook his head, chastising himself for comparing the two. Especially when the issue wasn't a comparison of Evie and Liz, but a comparison of Evie and Samantha's situations.

It broke his heart to think about Samantha not talking to him for ten years. Not just for himself, but for Samantha, too.

And he suddenly saw what Finn was doing. This was the last-ditch effort of a father who loved his daughter, but had never been good at showing it.

Chapter Five

"SO, YOUR DAD was surprised you were here?"

Evie placed the burgers she'd grilled on rolls while Jenna poured margaritas. Sofía had meetings that night with the contractor she was using to renovate the resort. Lauren had a date night. Evie was almost glad to get a chance to talk this out with only one other person. Sometimes having three opinions was overwhelming.

"He admitted he knew I was here. He just pretended he was surprised to see me at Pax's rental office, so he could look affronted. You've heard the saying that the best defense is a good offense? He pretended to be offended, upset we'd run into each other, so I couldn't yell at him for following me."

Jenna accepted the paper plate with her burger and handed Evie a margarita. They sat at the iron table with a bright blue umbrella.

"Why do you think he followed you?"

"He could have any one of a million reasons, but I've been traveling here for months since Lily's funeral and no one has cared or bothered me. It's peaceful and quiet here. He might simply want the privacy."

"But you don't think so?"

She sneaked a peek at Jenna. "I think he's here because he needs money for lawyers."

"Oh."

"I'd happily give it to him to get him to go away."

"Then maybe that's what you should do."

"Give him money?"

"Call his lawyers. Tell them you'll pay your dad's defense bill if they'll get him to leave."

Evie didn't like her father—he was sleek, ruthless, sometimes cruel. She also hadn't talked to him in a decade. But going behind his back to talk to his lawyers seemed unnecessarily mean. He might not be troubled by hurting her. But if she hurt him back, she'd be no better than he was.

"That's cold."

"He stole from your trust fund and all but abandoned you most of your childhood."

"It still seems cruel to call his lawyers instead of talking to him myself."

"So talk to him."

"I don't want to initiate a conversation. It would just feed his imagination. He'd think there was a chance for a reconciliation, and he'd never leave."

"You say he's going to be popping up all over town, edging his way into your life. Just wait until the first time he does that and take him aside, tell him you're arranging for his legal defense fund, then call the lawyers and tell them to set up enough meetings to get him out of Paradise Key."

"That's a great idea. The perfect idea!"

"Well, you might not think it's perfect when you realize it means you can't hide out in the beach house anymore."

Evie glanced at the art-deco door and sighed. "I'm here enough. I don't mind mingling a bit." She grinned. "Maybe we should head out to a bar after this?"

Jenna took a big bite of her burger, shaking her head. Once she swallowed, she said, "I have work tomorrow."

Evie winced. "I do, too. The new video is up. I need to check stats, answer email questions from the website, that kind of thing."

"But we could do lunch."

"Yes, lunch!"

The next two days, she had lunch with Jenna and Sofía. Not once did her father find her. Thursday night, she and Lauren had dinner at Scallywags. Still no dad sightings.

Friday night, she was sure the lure of tourist traffic would draw him out to the pier for drinks, but he was a no show.

She walked around town all day Saturday—still didn't spot him.

Sunday, she sat on the beach in the public area, watching the kite display put on by a vendor.

Monday, she wondered if he wasn't having his groceries delivered or bought by neighbors because she hadn't seen him anywhere.

By the time eight o'clock on Tuesday morning came

around, she was a nervous wreck, looking around corners, hoping to see her dad so she could get this conversation over with.

When Pax didn't show up on the boardwalk for the video shoot, her nerves hit critical mass. She stormed to JavaStop. He wasn't there. She marched to his office. Dotty shook her head. He hadn't been there either. Deciding to confront him where he lived, she headed to his house.

She knocked, but didn't give him time to answer. She opened the door and stormed inside, calling, "Hey! Isn't there a guy in this house who's supposed to be making a video?"

The place stayed silent. So quiet Evie got a creepy feeling. With slow, deliberate steps, she inched her way past the white tufted chairs in the dining area, into the empty kitchen, and back into the living room.

She was just about to call her friends to see if anyone had seen him… when Pax came down the stairs. He wore the shorts and T-shirt she needed, but something was off. His face—

"Are you wearing makeup?" She hid her snort of amusement by covering it with a cough.

Samantha peeked out from behind him. "I did it! Isn't it great? I found a video that demonstrates how makeup artists do up celebrities for television."

Pax sent her a pleading look.

Evie blinked rapidly, still trying to keep herself from

laughing. His already dark brows had been given more color and shaped. His cheeks bore two circles of red blush. The thick gloss on his lips caught the light of the foyer fixture and reflected it at her.

"It's…um… The thing is, Samantha…" She swallowed back a giggle. "We're shooting outside. The work you did on your dad looks like makeup for indoor shooting."

Samantha gasped. "Oh, I'll go look for another video!"

Pax caught her hand before she could spin away. "I've been doing these videos for a couple of months without makeup," he said, emphasizing the last two words.

"That's right," Evie quickly added. "These are supposed to be casual. Natural."

Samantha said, "There are lots of videos about keeping someone's face natural."

Pax sent Evie another pleading look.

She said, "Yes. But let's just get through today's shoot, then we'll talk about this. Pax, you might want to use some face cream to get that off."

He shot her a grateful look, then took the steps two at a time and disappeared down the hall.

"Are you coming with us, Samantha?"

She nodded. "I was going to bring this—" She displayed a case Evie suspected held as much makeup as the cosmetics counter at a department store. "But I'm guessing we won't need it."

"We probably won't."

Samantha took the case back to her room before racing down the stairs to stand beside Evie. "I love doing this."

"Watching your dad make the video?"

"Being part of things. This is the most boring summer."

"I hear you. My dad sent me to boarding school in the winter, then dumped me in Paradise Key every summer." She smiled. "But I made friends. Eventually, I looked forward to coming here every year."

Samantha sighed. "All my friends are either light-years ahead of me with boys or in the stone age. Nobody's interested in the same things I am."

"Like makeup?"

She shrugged. "Makeup. Boys. Clothes." She eyed Evie's jeans and T-shirt. "I wish I could make plain jeans and a T-shirt look sexy the way you do."

Evie's brain had stalled on the word *boys*, but Samantha saying *sexy* revived it. The kid was twelve and trying to be sexy?

"You're not too young for makeup. You're certainly not too young for great clothes, though at your age you should be trying to look more pretty than sexy. And boys? The trick to the whole boy thing is to start off as friends with them."

Samantha's eyes brightened. "Really?"

Evie winced. She had no experience with twelve-year-old girls, except she had once been one. She shouldn't have said anything. "Yes, but you know what? I'm probably the last person who should be giving advice."

"Why? You're like the coolest person I know."

Evie laughed. "Then you need to meet more people."

Pax returned, his face scrubbed clean. He jogged down the stairs and headed directly to the door, not looking at either her or Samantha. When he stepped onto the porch, she and Samantha scurried after him. He said nothing the entire walk. Samantha also stayed silent, so Evie did, too.

At the boardwalk, Samantha raced over to Dave.

The cameraman said, "How's it going? Want me to teach you how to set up a shot?"

The second Samantha was occupied, Pax turned on Evie. "You are taking her out for coffee and talking to her about makeup."

Evie bit back a laugh. "Why? She's already found her sources."

"Don't even! You might be able to look at videos about makeup and separate the good from the bad, but Samantha can't. She needs guidance."

"All right." She sucked in a breath. "The truth is she and I already started a bit of a conversation." She grimaced. "The subject of boys actually crept in."

"Boys?" His eyes about popped out of his head. "She's too young for boys!"

"Don't worry. I suggested she make friends with them first."

Pax scrubbed his hand across his mouth. "That doesn't sound too bad." His nose twitched. "I think I have eyeliner in my nostril."

She did laugh at that. "No, you don't."

"I feel like a clown."

"You got all the makeup off."

When he groaned, she said, "You look fine." She paused and smiled. "Wonderful, really." The little extra black around his lashes gave him a sexy look that caused her pulse to scramble.

He peeked at her. "Wonderful, huh?"

She held his gaze. The scramble in her veins slowed. Amazement filled her. All these months she'd been afraid of their attraction, but getting to know him was fun in the most natural way. She wasn't afraid. She was so interested in him that she was willing to break a few of her own dating rules. Especially since anything between them would be a fling. He was tied to Paradise Key, and her real life was in Philly.

The bottom line was this attraction between them was just a little too hard to ignore, and Lauren was right. Maybe they both needed a fling.

"Yes. You look wonderful."

Silence stretched between them. Thick and tight. If it was anybody else, she might have risen to her tiptoes and kissed him. But he was Pax. A good man. And she was a woman with too much money, an artificial home, and no family. A woman only looking for a fling.

It was no wonder he didn't want her.

Otherwise, he'd have said, "You look wonderful, too."

When he said nothing, embarrassment spilled through her. Needing to shift the conversation, she said, "You know, at least you spend time with your daughter. My dad was always shuttling me away. You let your daughter put makeup on your face." She grinned. "Before a video shoot."

"Yeah, well, I was an innocent led to slaughter. I didn't know any better. Now I do. Don't look for it to happen again."

Fear for Samantha filled her. "Don't stop doing things with her because of one little mistake."

"One little mistake? Our lives are changing. It's not like we can go outside to the backyard and play catch anymore. She wants different things. Girlie things."

Evie remembered a time when she was thirteen—not Samantha's age, but close—coming home from boarding school, eager to see her dad, and having him fumble his way through an awkward greeting, followed by an even more awkward supper. Thinking he didn't care about her, or what interested her, was the beginning of the end of their relationship.

But what if he'd been as uncomfortable as Pax?

And what if they'd had someone—like her, someone who'd lost her relationship with her dad—who could have helped them?

She took a sharp breath, reminding herself that her dad wasn't like Pax. Her father had stolen from her, gambled, and traveled in disreputable circles. Dealing in what-ifs about her dad was pointless.

But her experience still made her the perfect person to help Pax and Samantha. "Maybe when I come over to talk about the makeup, we can all do something together?"

"Like what?"

"Play Yahtzee?"

"Yahtzee?"

"It's a dice game. It requires enough brain power to be fun for an adult, but it's not so difficult that a twelve-year-old girl would be overwhelmed."

"I don't know."

"Hey, she put makeup on your face today. She loves being at these shoots. It proves she hasn't lost faith in you yet."

"Right."

"I'm serious. I know what it feels like when a little girl loses faith in her dad. She's not there yet. And you don't want her to get there."

He softened. "No. I don't."

"Okay, then. Trust me."

He nodded. "All right."

DAVE MOTIONED TO Evie that he was ready. Pax went to the designated starting point, but he caught a glimpse of himself in a store window and groaned.

He could still see the eyeliner. Evie assured him it wasn't

noticeable, but it messed with his confidence. He fumbled his way through seven takes before he finally got it right.

It wasn't just because his crazy brain kept telling him he looked like Prince on a bad day, but because he knew Evie was right. This was the point he had to grab his relationship his daughter and hold on for dear life.

And the one person who seemed to understand that, which also probably meant she knew how to help him do that, was the woman who drove him to distraction.

PAX WAS A nervous wreck on Wednesday night when Evie arrived to chat with Samantha and play Yahtzee.

He didn't like needing someone to help him, but needing someone as beautiful and seductive as Evie was a huge mistake. He'd considered having Dotty talk to Sam, but knew she didn't have the expertise or experience Evie did.

Even better though, Evie had connected with Samantha. He couldn't ignore this opportunity when so much was at stake.

He opened the door with a smile that even he knew had to look forced. "Hi."

She stepped into the foyer. "Hi."

"I hope you don't mind, but I took the liberty of marinating some steaks for supper."

Her head tilted. "Why would I mind?"

"I'm not sure when the makeup stuff will stop and the Yahtzee will begin." He ran his fingers through his hair. "It's the timing that has me befuddled." That and seeing her again, getting used to having her in his home, and trusting her with his precious daughter.

"Relax. This isn't a date. This is a little something we're doing for you and Samantha. How about you grill the steaks while she and I have a few minutes alone?"

Relief filled him. "That sounds great."

He called up the stairs for Samantha. "Evie's here!"

She came flying down. "I have my computer all set up in my room."

Evie displayed her makeup case. "I thought I'd bring this in case I have things you don't. Like something that washes off makeup. When I was your age, I was so focused on learning how to put makeup on I never once considered how to get it off."

"Cool!"

The urge to kiss Evie rose up in him, swift and hot. She had to be the sexiest woman on the face of the earth, yet she was so easygoing with Samantha.

As they climbed the stairs, he made his way through the dining room to the back deck, chastising himself for the foolish thought. Kiss Evie? And not just because she was a gorgeous temptress. Because she was a good person? A week ago, he never would have thought so, but it was true. She wasn't merely kind to his daughter. Helping Sam helped him. She was helping him, too.

He decided to label the urge to kiss her gratitude—had he kissed her, it would have been a gratitude kiss—and started grilling the veggies. Determined to forget it, he put the steaks on. Twenty minutes later, when everything was cooked, he returned to the foyer and called up the steps for Evie and Samantha.

Samantha came downstairs a different person. Polished. He suspected she was wearing makeup, but it was barely visible. He could have kissed Evie for that, too, and realized his answer for everything with Evie was to kiss her. It was wrong, ridiculously wrong. They came from two different worlds. He'd had his one great love, and it had ended in a great heartbreak. Evie had been through her share of misery, too. Why get involved when they knew it would end...and when it ended, they'd be hurt?

So...no kisses or thoughts of kisses.

He was glad when the Yahtzee game got competitive. Except when Sam pulled into the lead, she also started sighing.

"What's wrong?"

Sam sighed again. "It's boring. I'm beating your pants off because it's so easy. I can't believe you like this game."

"I like this game," Evie said with a laugh. "I never did anything like this when I was a kid."

"Well, it's kind of stupid. We throw dice and put our scores on a sheet." She rolled her eyes. "Bor-ing."

"Well, could we finish the game because our guest is enjoying it?" Pax asked, annoyed with the fact Sam only seemed to be seeing things her way lately.

"Sure," Sam said sullenly. "We'll finish for Evie."

Suddenly, Pax saw it.

Twelve might not be very old, but his little girl was tiptoeing toward her teen years and the horrible R word. Rebellion.

He knew what happened with teenagers. They slipped into a few years of hating school, hating life...hating their parents. And Sam was on the cusp of that.

He spent the rest of the evening alternating between brooding over Samantha growing up too fast and trying to avoid accidentally touching Evie's hand when he reached for the dice.

When the game was finished, Sam bounced off her seat and headed for the stairs. "I have to check Instagram before I shower for bed."

He watched her race up the steps and out of his sight.

"You're not going to lose her."

He faced Evie. "How do you know?"

"Because you try with her. I understood my dad was grieving my mom, but so was I. His answer to everything was to ship me away. He made boarding school seem like it was going to be one long party." She cut Pax a look. "It wasn't, by the way. He brought me down here every summer and all but abandoned me for parties, fishing trips, and afternoons with friends."

She sighed and walked over to the stairway where she'd stashed her makeup case. She picked it up with a long exhale of breath.

"You know what? I'm sorry that all I seem to do with you is complain about my father."

Standing by the door, waiting to open it for her, he shook his head. "Honestly, I'm glad for the warning."

"Yeah, I know the saying about a person's life being a good example or a dire warning. It's really fun to be cast in the dire-warning category."

He could see in her soft gray eyes that it hurt her. His gut clenched with regret. "I didn't mean that like it sounded. But I'm not going to lie and say you're not helping me. You are. And I appreciate it."

The light returned to her eyes again, causing relief to course through him. But staring into her eyes resurrected the desire to kiss her. Would one kiss really be so wrong?

No.

Yes!

Her lips tilted up, and warmth raced to his toes.

Damn it, who cared if it was right or wrong? It was what they both wanted.

He bent his head as she angled hers toward him, confirmation they were feeling the same thing. When their lips met, he swore he felt a zap of electricity followed by a flood of warmth. That should have been another kind of warning.

Instead, temptation took the place of common sense. He caught her upper arms and pulled her to him, moving his lips against hers before deepening the kiss so he could taste her.

"Dad, Sylvia Johnson is on Instagram saying something about the water in the house she rents from you being bad."

The sound was distant, as if Sam was shouting from her room, but he jumped away from Evie like a guilty teenager. She blinked her eyes open slowly, as if in a daze.

He envied that. The antidote for arousal, Samantha's voice dragged him back to the real world by the scruff of his neck.

He called, "I'm coming!" up the stairs, then faced a wide-eyed Evie.

"I'm sorry. I shouldn't have done that."

She blinked again, still working to get her bearings. "Sorry?"

"We're oil and water, remember? Plus, you're leaving and I'm staying." He shook his head. "Kissing you was foolish."

Chapter Six

EVIE STARED UP at him in disbelief. That was probably the best kiss she'd ever had...and he was sorry?

Her pride suffered a direct hit. But as she always did when someone hurt her, she recovered quickly. She reminded herself that she didn't need anybody. That she could and did make it on her own. It didn't take away the pain, but it made it manageable.

He pointed toward the back door in the kitchen. "I've gotta get my tools."

She cleared her throat. "Yeah. Sure. I understand Go see what's wrong with that woman's water."

She stepped out into the humid night and wandered up the street. Paradise Key managed to maintain a small-town atmosphere, even as the nightclubs, restaurants, and bars near the pier area were probably rocking.

Her pride still stinging, she considered going over to the pier, getting a drink, seeing if anyone she knew was around, but her brain immediately vetoed the idea. As alone as she felt, she didn't want company. She might be able to make it on her own, but an insult was an insult and it hurt. Maybe tomorrow, she'd call her friends. Tonight, she wanted to lick her wounds in private.

She went home, to the beautiful beach house Pax had rented to her. As the light flickered on, she looked around at the design, the way the stylish furnishings and fixtures were also practical. Once again, she had the sense that Pax's wife was there with her.

In a way, she was. Every item in every room spoke of her taste in design. Evie didn't think too much of it until her thoughts turned to that kiss.

What was she doing thinking about kissing a woman's husband when she felt that woman's presence all over her home?

She shook her head, telling herself to forget the kiss because that was never going to happen again, but she had the strangest sense her thought was wrong. That she should give Pax another chance. Or maybe time—

She laughed. Was she arguing with herself?

Maybe.

That kiss had been amazing, and Pax was wonderful. But he was also right. She was leaving. He was staying. And their personalities didn't mesh. They were something like oil and water.

Plus, Evie Barclay didn't argue with herself. When someone didn't want her, she knew how to move on.

But Samantha did want to spend time with her, and she knew Pax was correct about something else. If someone didn't help his daughter understand the changes in her life, she'd flounder through her teen years, just as Evie had.

The next morning, Evie was going over the emails received on the town's website, answering the ones with easy questions, and forwarding others to the visitor's bureau, when Samantha called.

"What are you doing today?"

Samantha's voice was so light, so airy, so happy that it immediately lifted Evie's mood. "Nothing. You have any ideas?"

"I don't know. I'm kind of bored."

Bored. Again. Evie remembered that part of childhood very well.

"We could have lunch. Afterward, we could read fashion magazines on my back deck."

"All right!"

"I'll come by your house around noon to get you."

After Evie finished her work, she popped over to Sam's house, leading her to one of the restaurants on the boardwalk. "For exercise," Evie told Samantha. "Little tip. If you're not the kind of person who likes going to a gym—"

Samantha grimaced. "I'm not."

"Then it's very easy to get exercise into your day by walking."

"Walking?"

Evie put her face up and soaked in the noonday sun. "You notice I didn't rent a car?"

Samantha's lips twisted as she thought about that.

"I didn't," Evie said, ending her confusion. Twelve-year-old girls were smart and funny, but Sam wasn't an adult. Which was part of the appeal. Evie had wished with all her heart for someone to step in and help her with things like makeup, diets, and boys. No matter that Pax didn't want anything to do with her, she'd never abandon Sam. "I'm using walking around town for coffee or lunch or dinner or to shop as the way to get my exercise in for the day."

Sam said, "Cool."

"I think so." Evie opened the door of the local pizza place, and cold air hit them.

Sam shivered. "We should have brought a sweater."

Evie batted a hand. "We'll get used to it."

"Okay."

"Okay."

They found a small table in the back, ordered a large pizza and water—another Evie tip. Calories shouldn't be wasted on drinks—and spent a fun hour chitchatting about birds on the beach, the value of a backyard swimming pool, and how some of Samantha's school friends would like to meet Evie.

Evie frowned. "I'll think about it. But, you know, things like makeup parties can get a little awkward. It would be a lot simpler if we just accidentally ran into them one at a time on the street."

Sam nodded eagerly. "Okay."

Evie rose from the table. "Like right now. We'll walk back to your house to use up some of that pizza we just ate.

If we just happen to run into one or two of your friends, I can meet them."

"Hey, Pax. Look out your office window."

Knowing Dotty only gave him orders like that for good reasons, Pax rose from his desk, opened the blinds, and chuckled.

Evie Barclay stood in the center of a cluster of Sam's friends, looking like a tour guide as she directed them down the street.

"What's she doing?" Dotty asked from his doorway.

With a shake of his head, he faced his assistant. "I have no idea. But Sam adores her. If Evie's willing to make time to help her with girlie things, I'm not arguing."

"She's an interesting person."

Though Pax wouldn't disagree, he didn't want to talk about Evie. She'd haunted his dreams, made him feel bad about dismissing her, and caused him to feel lower than low because she should be mad at him, but she wasn't. Instead, she led Sam and her friends around town like a mother duck.

"Yes. She's interesting."

But seeing his daughter staring at Evie with stars in her eyes gave Pax the oddest sense. He might have found a way for Sam to grow and be comfortable with who she was and even learn about girlie things, but *he* wasn't involved.

Evie was. She wasn't linking them together. Giving Samantha someone to talk to other than him might actually tear them apart.

He spent the weekend brooding about that, not really finding any avenues to work his way into his daughter's life. Though he tried. He suggested fishing. She gaped at him as if he were crazy. He suggested they go to the beach. She already had plans to go with her friends.

He found himself alone and bored most of Saturday and all of Sunday.

On Monday night, he remembered he had to make a video the next morning. He groaned. With all the stuff going on with Samantha, as well as working to avoid an attraction to a woman who wasn't merely all wrong for him, but also would be leaving town soon, the last thing he wanted to do was make a video.

He called Lauren's cell phone and got voice mail. "Hey, Lauren, Pax. Listen, I've mentioned to Evie a few times that I no longer want…" He paused and shook his head. This wasn't a matter of want. It was a matter of need. "I can't do the video anymore. Between my job as mayor, the Paxton Properties work, and my stuff with my daughter, I'm booked. I'll be happy to meet with you tomorrow at eight and discuss a replacement, but I've made my last video."

EVIE WAS AWAKENED at six-thirty the next morning by a text beep. Bleary-eyed, she grabbed for the phone and saw a message from Lauren.

Pax doesn't want to do the video anymore.

Before Evie could remind herself that she was supposed to be relieved not to have to see the guy who was sorry he kissed her, her chest tightened. They'd had fun Wednesday night. Normal fun. They'd done the kinds of things she'd always known families did, but she'd never had the pleasure of trying. And now he wanted out of the video—away from her—because she'd eventually be leaving town? Because she wasn't like his wife? Because he didn't want their attraction?

She sat up in bed. It could be all of them. And she couldn't blame him. She wasn't a homespun designer who loved to make soup. She was....

These days, she wasn't quite sure what she was. She loved keeping up the town's website and making that stupid video almost as much as she did her talk show. Mostly because she wasn't the boss. She was part of a team. Everybody talked to her like an equal. She didn't have the burden of responsibility. She had work she did that was fun and important. But everybody at the PR firm did. They all talked to each other. Supported each other.

She also liked being involved with Samantha. She loved being around Sam's friends—and her own friends.

She was even getting accustomed to having sand between

her toes.

Her phone pinged again.

Sorry about that. I got a bit distracted.

Evie laughed. She'd probably gotten distracted by Carter Malone.

Anyway, Pax wants a meeting this morning. So instead of going to the boardwalk, come to my office.

Evie jumped out of bed. She was tired of ignoring their attraction and tired of Pax calling all the shots, albeit by avoiding her. So he had a daughter? So he'd suffered losses? She'd had losses, too. Plenty of them. Enough to know life went on. If he wanted to spend the rest of his life in mourning, she'd certainly let him. But she refused to feel bad for being attracted to him.

Or for him being attracted to her.

A thought hit her, and she laughed. Scrambling out of bed, she headed to her closet.

She arrived at Lauren's office at five till eight, only to find Pax and Lauren already in the conference room.

She sucked in a breath, straightening her blouse. She wouldn't say she'd dressed special for this meeting, but she wasn't wearing jeans and a T-shirt. Instead, she had on wedge sandals, a flowing skirt, and a reasonably low-cut blouse. Not trashy. Evie Barclay didn't do trashy. But she had no problem with sexy.

Carrying her tablet, she strolled into the conference room. "Good morning."

Lauren spun her chair around. "Hey, good morning!"

Pax rose. "Good morning."

His eyes dipped to her blouse for only a second, but enough for Evie to have to stifle a giggle. Pretend to hate his attraction to her? Avoid her like the plague? She'd show him.

She took a seat across from him. "Why the meeting?"

Lauren said, "Pax doesn't want to do the video anymore."

Her business demeanor in place, Evie said, "I don't know why." She caught his gaze and held it. "You're very good at it."

"Last week, we had to do seven takes." He shook his head. "*Seven takes* for reading a list."

"In fairness, you don't read that list. You memorize it." Refusing to break eye contact, she added, "And you improvise a great deal. You have a touch of something. A talent, I guess, for making that video seem real and alive. It's like talking to you."

"It's a pain in the butt."

"That may be so," Lauren said, "But we get a great deal of response to it."

Evie's phone pinged again. Curious, she surreptitiously tapped the screen to read the text from Samantha.

Dad's not here. Are we meeting at the boardwalk for the shoot? I know it's a bit late, but Dad will do enough takes that I should get there before the last one.

Evie bit her lip as Lauren went on about market shares and click-to-reservation ratios.

Pax shook his head. "I can't be the reason."

"You *are* the reason," Lauren insisted. "You're the face of the town. People love you."

"Last I heard, people were making memes. Laughing at me."

"*At your hair*," Evie put in. "And just that one week. It never happened again because Samantha always brings a comb."

He scowled.

"And speaking of Samantha." Evie slid her phone across the desk to him. "She's looking for us."

Pax glanced at the text message, then his eyes rose to meet Evie's.

"She likes making this video. *With you*. She may not want to play games with you anymore or go fishing. She's outgrown both of those, and her interests are now in things she doesn't want to discuss with you. But she sure likes making this video, feeling part of things, keeping your hair neat."

He said nothing. Lauren sent Evie a questioning look. She returned it with a please-trust-me expression.

Pax slid Evie's phone back to her. "She does seem to enjoy this."

"It's a way to connect and stay connected. It might even

turn into a career," Evie said. "She might go from wanting to be the person who keeps you looking good to someone who understands the actual filming process, and then who knows? Maybe she'll start writing scripts."

Lauren laughed. "And then she'll be working for me."

Pax drew a breath.

Evie said, "I know this disrupts your schedule. But for the sake of your relationship with Sam, I think it's worth it."

"All right."

Lauren's face brightened. "Really? You're back on board?"

"Yes. Because Evie's right. Sam loves this, and I love Sam. I'm not ready to lose her to makeup and boys and Snapchat and Instagram or whatever they come up with next on the internet."

Lauren stood, beaming. "Good."

Evie said, "I'll text Sam and tell her to meet us on the boardwalk."

"Okay. I'll see you there."

Typing into her phone, Evie said, "No sense going separately. Give me two seconds." She finished her text and grinned. "See? Ready. Let's go."

They stepped out into the early morning sunshine and Evie tried to think of something to say. But she had nothing. If she knew exactly what she wanted from Pax, she'd either flirt or talk or just be herself with him. But while part of her thought Pax should be off limits and another thought she should flirt her heart out until he melted at her feet, a third raised its head and said the man should be trying to persuade *her* to like *him*, not the other way around.

After all, he was the one who'd kissed her.

"How are you going to walk in the sand in those things?" He pointed at her shoes. "And in a dress."

"It's not a dress. It's a skirt."

"It's going to fly up in the first breeze."

"That's actually the point of wearing a gauzy skirt. It's light and airy to catch the breeze."

He shot her a horrified glance. "So people can see your business?"

She almost choked at the way he said it, as if he were afraid of intimate apparel.

"If you mean panties, then no. The skirt is layered. Not all the layers fly up at once. No panties will be seen this morning."

His face changed. His expression worsened before he turned away from her and headed toward the boardwalk.

The devil returned to tempt her, and she scurried after him. "Disappointed you're not going to see my panties?"

"No."

"Yes, you are. You might not want to admit you're interested. It might not fit your five-year plan. But you like what you see. And let's not forget who kissed whom."

"I said I was sorry."

"Oh, yes. An apology after a kiss is what every woman

wants."

He didn't reply, and she tried not to seethe. The man liked her. Why couldn't he just admit it?

Sam was waiting for them when they reached the boardwalk. Dave stood in his usual spot, fiddling with his camera for the perfect light settings.

Pax didn't say anything, just marched to his regular starting place.

After a few seconds of discussion to make sure everyone was ready, Dave counted down, "Five, four, three, two, one..." and pointed at Pax.

"Good morning from beautiful Paradise Key, Florida." He opened his arms. "As you can see, it's a glorious day. This week..."

The breeze blew, raising the first layer of Evie's skirt.

He faltered. "This week, we have three special events."

Evie said, "Cut."

Sighing, Pax said, "Why?"

"Because you repeated this week. You stumbled over your words."

He cleared his throat. "Okay. Fine. Let's do it again."

He returned to his place, but Evie laughed to herself. He might not want to admit he was attracted to her, but he paid a hell of a lot of attention to her if noticing her skirt in the breeze was what had caused him to stumble over his words.

Dave said, "Five, four, three, two, one..." He pointed at Pax.

"Good morning from beautiful Paradise Key, Florida." He opened his arms. "As you can see, it's a glorious day. This week…"

Temptation overcame her again, and she deliberately dropped her pen. It fell soundlessly into the white sand. She bent to pick it up, not necessarily displaying her cleavage. That would have been tacky. But simply calling attention to her blouse.

Pax tripped over his words again.

Dave called, "Cut," as Evie put her hand over her lips to hide her giggle.

Pax glared at her.

She batted her lashes. "What?"

He rolled his eyes and headed back to his starting spot.

Evie also changed positions. Instead of standing beside Samantha, who was next to Dave, she ambled to the railing on Pax's left, out of view of the shot, but close enough that he'd have to walk by her. She leaned her bottom against the railing, balanced her hands on either side of her butt, and let her hair fly in the wind as she watched him.

"Good morning from beautiful Paradise Key, Florida." He opened his arms. "As you can see, it's a glorious day. This week, we have two very special events."

She smirked and said, "Cut. We have three."

He cursed, and she pushed away from the railing. She walked over to him with a smile and whispered, "Never lie to me again. But most of all, never lie to yourself."

She went back to her place beside Dave and Sam. Dave counted down. Pax started his spiel. He didn't make a mistake until almost the end.

Evie said, "Cut."

More subdued than she'd ever seen him, he started over. That take was the last one.

She gathered her tablet and pencil, getting ready to leave.

Pax approached her. He glanced at Sam, who was chatting with Dave, then at Evie. "Are you coming over tonight?"

She saw the direction of Pax's gaze, and a funny feeling tightened her chest. Evie could flirt with him all she wanted, and he would resist her. All he really needed from her was help with Sam. Maybe it was time she admitted that.

She shored up her determination. And maybe it was time to go back into Evie Barclay protection mode. "I probably won't be over tonight."

"Are you busy?"

"Not really." It dawned on her that this wasn't just about her and Pax. Samantha was part of the mix. She couldn't refuse if Sam needed her.

She faced Pax's daughter. "Is there something you need? A new video you found?"

Sam shrugged. "No. But there are a few things I want to talk about, so I think you should come over for dinner."

Evie laughed. "If it's just you and me, I say we go to a nice restaurant."

"No, with Dad!"

There was the tiniest note of desperation in Sam's voice, but it was enough for Evie to see what was going on. Pax's little girl was matchmaking.

"Can't you make burgers, Dad?"

He sighed. "Honey, Miss Barclay might have other things to do."

Miss Barclay? Evie had to hold back a chuckle. Pax was fighting his attraction so much he was losing it. And having his daughter play matchmaker was like a stamp of approval on the relationship. Maybe Evie was bored, but suddenly dinner with him trying to pretend he wasn't interested in her seemed like fun.

"Nope. My schedule's free as a bird."

Sam spun to face her dad. "See! She can come." She paused. Eventually, with some reluctance, she said, "I'll even play a game."

Her dad looked skeptical. "A board game?"

Sam groaned. "How about cards?"

He glanced at Evie. "Do you play cards?"

Suddenly the situation wasn't about making Pax squirm. It was about Pax getting time with Sam. "I love cards."

Looking relieved, Pax said, "Great. See you at six."

Chapter Seven

PAX LEFT THE shoot so confused his head spun. On one hand, it was pure pleasure to watch gorgeous Evie in the flowing skirt, her skin shining in the sun, her hair blowing in the breeze. It had also been great to see Sam interested in having Evie over for dinner. She even wanted to play cards.

On the other hand, Evie had been flirting with him. Hardcore. He'd managed to ignore it while they were shooting, but when she gave him that look just now, instincts he hadn't had in five years had awoken to yawn and stretch and come fully alive.

For the first time since, Liz's death, it hadn't seemed wrong to be interested in another woman. It had seemed...like it was time. Time to stop mourning and move on.

Yet, that didn't seem right either. He didn't feel he was betraying Liz by being interested in Evie. It was more he felt Liz slipping away.

He pushed open the door to JavaStop and was greeted by Lorelei. "Morning, Mayor. Which scone will it be today?"

He peered at the pastries behind the glass. "I'm thinking I want a muffin."

"Oh, oh. What's Tyson done now?"

He pointed at a particularly fat muffin with plump blueberries bulging out. "Nothing. Why would you think Tyson did something?"

"Well, muffins are your go-to pastry when you're flummoxed."

He gaped at her. Given that Tyson was her boyfriend, he didn't want her thinking the flimsy bureaucrat could unnerve him. "I don't get flummoxed."

"Sure, you do."

She busied herself getting his coffee and grabbing the muffin. As always, she tried to wave away his money, but he insisted on paying.

He turned from the counter and saw Finn Barclay, sitting in the corner on the sofa, folding a newspaper to get himself to the appropriate page and article.

Common sense told Pax to run, but as he headed for the door, Finn saw him.

"Hey, Mr. Mayor! Why not come over and have a cup of coffee with a guy who could use a little company?"

Damn.

If Finn hadn't sounded like the most dejected man on the face of the earth, Pax might have ignored him. But he did sound lonely. A state Pax would probably find himself in a few years, after Samantha left for college, then made a place for herself in the world.

He sighed, saddened for himself, too, and made his way

to the sofa and chair arrangement. He set his coffee and muffin on the table. "What are you reading?"

"A little about the state of my arrest. *USA Today* seems to think I'm going away for a long time. *The Wall Street Journal* reporter is making a case for the fact that I'm hiding something." He leaned closer. "Or protecting my friends."

"Which is it?"

Finn leaned back against the sofa. "I think I'm going to jail for a long time."

"How did you get the info…the insider trading tips?"

Finn laughed. "And therein lies my defense."

"Oh." Finally something good for this poor, dejected guy. "Is it anything you can't talk about?"

"No." Finn paused. "I would, however, like to talk about you and my daughter on the boardwalk this morning."

Pax winced. "I hate that damned video."

"I've seen it. It's cute. I can tell the point when my daughter took over because you appear to be trying harder." He caught Pax's gaze. "Another sign that you like her."

"Look, she's a very attractive woman, but—"

"But what? She's not good enough for you?"

Pax laughed. "She's too good for me. I'm a widower." He patted his chest. "I still have a broken heart." No matter how strong his instincts, he couldn't bear the thought of Liz slipping away.

"Ah. The old broken heart routine."

Pax raised a brow. "It's not a routine."

"You're right. After a while, it becomes a crutch."

"It's not a crutch!"

"Which takes us back to you thinking you're too good for my daughter. I saw how she looked at you today, son. Saw the flirting. And saw you ignoring her."

"Then you missed the fact that we did about seven takes. She is not that easy to ignore."

Finn chuckled. "She never was. Heart of gold and big, sad eyes like a kitten." He shook his head. "You can't believe how I miss her."

"So what happened?"

"Happened?"

"How did you lose her? I have a twelve-year-old daughter on the brink of shutting me out of her life."

"Don't want to make the same mistake I did?"

Pax nodded.

"Don't take a chunk of her trust fund."

Pax considered for a second, but in the end, his curiosity won out. "That was stupid, and you don't seem like a stupid man."

"I wasn't. At least, I didn't think I was."

"So…"

"I was losing the house. Picture this…I'm a twenty-two-year-old actor with a halfway decent career who marries a woman who has never had to consider the value of a dollar. We bought a big house in Connecticut, cars for every occasion, and had a beautiful daughter whom we spoiled like it was a religion."

Pax said nothing.

"Anyway, Annie and her dad are killed in an airplane accident. Drunk pilot they said, which didn't help me one whit. I spent a year in horrible, dark grief. When I came out, I was losing the house."

"Why?"

"Taxes. I hadn't worked in a year. My old movie residuals weren't even six figures, and they were dwindling. I lived in a champagne world and anything under mid-six-figures was a beer-barrel income. I pulled myself together, got the information from my deceased father-in-law's accountants who were getting the tax notices, water bills, and everything else, but not paying them because all the money went to Evie. The Jones fortune was slapped into a trust before her grandfather was even in the ground."

"You're saying you got into trouble because of grief?"

"I got into trouble because I was broke. I might have made a couple million a year when I was working steadily, but being Mr. Anna Jones-Barclay was a full-time job." He shook his head. "I'm not making excuses, just explaining why I mortgaged the house. I tried to get work, couldn't, and ended up on the verge of losing everything."

"That's when you took money from the trust?"

"That's when I *legally* took money from the trust."

"You took some illegally?"

"Eventually." He shrugged. "It looked legal, but I'd lied.

Inflated things like the cost of Evie's private schools. By the time anyone got onto me, I'd spent about half her money."

Pax didn't know exact figures, but he'd guess Evie had been worth upward of a billion dollars. "That's a chunk of change."

"It costs a lot to make a little girl accustomed to having the world at her feet believe everything's fine."

"You should have talked to her."

Finn shook his head. "She'd lost her mom. As the years went on, she missed her more, not less. And I was a schlepp. I gambled. I drank. I'd clean up and hire a maid for the weeks she'd be home, but as soon as she was gone, I'd close up the house and go on a bender." He paused, sighed. "I'm sober now, but she doesn't know that."

Pax said nothing.

"Every time she'd come home from boarding school, I'd think this is the year it's all going to fall apart, but it wouldn't, and I'd consider it a sign I should keep going. But when Evie turned twenty-one and the trust reverted to her, she found the discrepancies. She knew what I'd done."

"Did you tell her, explain the façade?"

"At the time, I had a little more pride than brains. Besides, she knew she'd paid for gambling junkets." He rose. "I made this bed I'm lying in. The insider trading? It was my last-ditch attempt to get respectable again. To have enough money that we would be on even terms and maybe I could even pay some back. But interestingly, now that I'm nothing but a broke alcoholic, I don't have a scam, don't have a plan. I just know my wife would be ashamed of me. And I need to fix that."

He headed for the door and Pax watched him, filled with sadness. Finn had done all the wrong things for all the right reasons. He'd been fueled by grief and a huge amount of fear, all egged on by alcohol. Pax had gone in the opposite direction. He'd thrown himself into work, made money, made something of himself. But the temptation had always been there to wallow in the grief. To rail at the universe for taking away the woman he loved, the life he'd had planned.

He wouldn't judge.

WHEN EVIE SHOWED up at his house that night at six, Pax let her in with a big smile. Probably too big. He'd listened to her dad talk that afternoon because he didn't want to end up losing his daughter the way Finn had lost his. But now Pax wished he didn't know Finn's misery, his regret for what he'd done.

It was also a bit of a stab to the ego that Finn accused him of using the loss of his wife as a crutch.

He'd dated.

But not seriously.

He'd certainly never felt for a woman what he felt every second he was around Evie.

Especially tonight. She wore an airy blue top and white jeans with the same wedge-heeled shoes she'd had on that morning at the video shoot. But the show-stopper was her hair. Always her hair. She had gorgeous yellow hair, thick with fat curls that bounced when she walked or shook her head. It made him long to run his fingers through it.

He cleared his throat as he motioned for her to step inside. "No makeup case today?"

She raised her empty hands. "I texted Sam. She said we didn't need it tonight."

"Okay. More time for cards then."

She smiled. Not a flirty smile. An almost-empty smile. If she'd felt something for him, it was long gone, or she'd decided to suppress it. Probably because the only way he'd seemed interested in her was for help with Sam. "More time for cards," she agreed.

His heart plummeted. He was finally getting what he wanted from her. She was leaving him alone. But wretchedness rattled through him. Not just for the way he seemed to be using her, but for her personally. After his talk with her father, he pictured her alone a lot, with a dad who couldn't talk to her, be honest with her, because he didn't want to be a disappointment.

Still, what could Pax do about that? Nothing. He had to stay out of it.

"Can I get you a drink?"

"If we're having burgers, a beer would be great."

He'd pictured her asking for something fancy like a Cosmopolitan or very dry martini. When she asked for a beer, he realized again just how little he knew her.

"We are having burgers on the patio out back. And I do have beer."

He paused at the stairway and called, "Samantha, Evie's here!"

Samantha's, "Okay, Dad!" flowed down the stairs.

He directed Evie to the sliding glass doors in the kitchen. The scent of the grilling burgers wafted to them as he opened the door and motioned for her to exit first.

Evie looked around at the dark wood island containing a gas grill. The slab of gray granite for the countertop was the same as the granite in his kitchen. A long, reclaimed wood table gleamed in the late day sun. Surrounded by thickly padded barrel chairs, it sat eight. The bright aqua and blue area rug beneath the table pulled it all together under an inconspicuous roof that protected the space from both sun and rain. The house sat close to neighbors, but no one had erected a fence. They liked each other. Respected each other. Had a few beers together in the winter when they built fires in pits in the backs of their yards.

"Nice patio." She turned to him with a smile. "Let me guess. Your wife designed this."

Surprised her mention of Elizabeth hadn't given him a ping of pain in his heart, he said, "No. I actually bought this house the year after Liz passed. I needed a little something to keep me busy. The remodel took two years."

"What did you do with Samantha while you worked?"

And there it was. The hurt her father had inflicted wobbled through her voice.

"We did this together. When we started, she was eight. I taught her to measure wood." He laughed and grabbed two beers from the small refrigerator built into the island. "Measure twice. Cut once. Ask her about it. She'll groan."

"I guess when it comes to remodeling, measuring twice and cutting once is probably a good idea."

"She'd turned ten by the time the house was finished. But she'd also become my best helper. I taught her to lay tile."

Taking her bottle of beer, Evie grinned. "Seriously?"

"She's very good with her hands. She did the low-level tiles in all the bathroom showers." He grimaced. "I wouldn't let her on a ladder."

Evie nodded. As she took a long swig of her beer, she surveyed the patio and yard again. This time, Pax could tell she was really seeing it.

"It's why you kept it."

"Could have gotten a pretty penny if I'd sold it, but the house was filled with memories."

"My father sold our house that was filled with our memories."

What should have been an innocent comment almost stopped Pax's heart. Had she known her dad couldn't afford the house? Had she even suspected? Or had her father protected her so much that he let himself take her anger rather than look like a failure to her?

He fought the urge to ask, but the words eventually tumbled out. "When did he sell it?"

She took a seat at the table on one of the barrel chairs. "When I went to college." She took another swing of beer. "He said it was too big and empty."

A plausible cover. "Maybe it was."

"The house was filled with books. My mom's books. Had he given me a chance, I would have taken some of those. And her vanity, an antique from my great-grandmother. I wanted that, but he sold it with the house."

Pax winced. Selling the house was one thing. Not telling her until it was a done deal wasn't very wise. Not letting her take a memento or two had been just plain stupid. But Pax wasn't sure he'd have been smart enough to realize Samantha might want some of Liz's things, if his sister hadn't set some aside.

Of course, by the time Finn sold his house, his wife had been dead quite a few years and Evie had been a lot older. He should have been able to talk to her.

Pax shook his head, not knowing what to think. For as much as he empathized with Finn, he would like to believe he'd have thought some of this through better than Finn had.

"I have a lot of her jewelry."

His head snapped up when Evie spoke. "Well, that's good."

"But it was the intangibles that killed me."

"Intangibles?"

"Our living room held the best reminders of Christmases. My mom loved making apple pancakes in the kitchen. If I close my eyes, I can still picture it. We had great dinner parties in a dining room the size of a ballroom." She caught his gaze. "Had I known he was selling that house, I would have bought it."

And probably discovered a few years sooner that her dad was using her trust fund and floundering financially.

But maybe that would have been a good thing?

He checked the hamburgers. "These are done. Would you mind coming into the kitchen with me to get the veggies and dip, while I call for Samantha again?"

She rose from the table. "I'm happy to do that."

Because she was a normal person.

Her name might be recognized around the world. Her story might be common knowledge. But when her guard was down, Evie Barclay was a sweet, unassuming woman.

Whose dad had crushed her.

He opened the patio door for her, and she entered before him. While she headed to the refrigerator, he strode through the kitchen and back down the hall to the stairway.

"Samantha! Dinner's ready."

She appeared at the top of the stairs and began jogging

down the steps, her tablet tucked under her arm. "Sorry, Dad. Big Instagram crisis. Someone has a picture of Olivia crying after a science test. She failed the test. That's why she's crying. But everybody's saying Brock Foster had broken up with her."

Pax's head spun. "He was her boyfriend?"

Samantha rolled her eyes. "They weren't dating. They only walked to classes together." She ran to the door. "We're all going to her house, so we can coordinate our posts to defend her."

He gaped as he watched her race out the front door.

Carrying the veggies and dip, Evie came into the foyer. "Did I just hear the door closing?"

Staring at the art-deco glass, he said, "Apparently, there's an Instagram crisis."

She laughed. "Instagram crisis?"

"Someone posted a picture. Another person made a comment that wasn't true, so a bunch of them are getting together to coordinate posts."

Evie's left eyebrow rose.

"They take this stuff very seriously."

"I know." Evie turned back toward the kitchen. "I read somewhere that platforms like Instagram, Facebook, Snap-Chat, and even Google Plus extend school time. Not the learning part, but the social part. And it's like kids don't get a rest from it."

She reached the back door and slid it open. Pax followed

her.

"Is that good or bad?"

"The report said it's good in some ways because it offers opportunities to form relationships more quickly. But bad in others because if there's a feud or a fight going on, kids don't have any time away from it. There's no safe haven at home anymore. In the middle of the night, a phone or tablet can ping with a message and they're back in it again."

She set the veggies on the table. Pax retrieved placemats, plates, and utensils from one of the cupboards in the island. He brought them over and distributed them before taking the hamburgers from the grill.

He winced. "Forgot the buns."

After racing into the kitchen to get them, he set them on the table, telling Evie to dig in. He took his seat, fixed his burger, grabbed some veggies, and then blinked.

Either he and Evie had gotten so comfortable with each other, or Samantha leaving had been so abrupt, but it took him until now to realize he and Evie were alone…

Chapter Eight

E VIE DUG INTO her burger. "Oh, this is fabulous."

"Yours isn't the only family that has things they pass down. Mine has recipes."

"I thought your mom was an actress?"

"My grandmother wasn't. She made the best guacamole. Wait till you taste it."

As Pax said the words, his eyes widened as if he'd realized he'd just hinted they'd be together again.

Evie shook her head in dismay. The man really thought a little too highly of himself. "Don't worry. I know it's just an expression."

He shrugged sheepishly. "I'm sorry. I'm not very good at this."

"At what?"

"At whatever is happening between us. If Samantha had been here, we'd be laughing, planning to play cards. Now—"

"Now nothing has changed. I mean, we don't have to play cards. But we didn't set out for this to be a date." Sheesh. Talk about a blow to an ego. This was guy killing her. "We're only friends. You made that abundantly clear this morning."

He winced. "Sorry about that."

"Don't be sorry! If you don't stop bumbling around me, I'm not going to have any ego left when I finally get to go back to Philly."

"I hurt your ego?"

"Seriously? You're a man who hates that he's attracted to me. You can't think I'm ugly or you wouldn't be attracted to me, but that leaves all kinds of things. Like you hate my personality. Or don't like who I am. Or maybe it bothers you that I have more money than you. To save my pride, I tell myself you hate being attracted to me because you're still devoted to your wife. But like I said, that's just me trying to save a little pride."

"That is the reason."

Relief poured through her. She set her burger down. "Really?"

"Yes. Come on, you're beautiful, smart, good with people. I saw how you rallied your friends after Lily's death. Dave likes you. Sam adores you. But I come with baggage."

"We all come with baggage."

"Not like mine."

Not proud of her curiosity, Evie nonetheless said, "Tell me about her." She picked up her burger, pretending the comment had been offhand. Simple. Not the big, curiosity-filled question it really was.

"Well, she was beautiful. But in a different way than you are."

Evie swallowed a bite of burger, trying not to get excited over the fact he'd complimented her again.

"She was a school teacher when we met. I'd come to Paradise Key for the same reason you had."

"To reunite with friends?"

"No. Your dad brought you here during the summer to give you something to do. I came for the same reason. I'd researched the resort, needed somewhere to live without buying a house, and thought this would give me a good transition place."

"Why'd you need to transition?"

He squeezed his eyes shut. "Failed sitcom."

She laughed. "What?"

"I told you. My mom wasted her first vat of money trying to develop something for herself. Another show. When that failed, she tried to develop something for my sister or me. Both of those shows bombed, too."

"And you were embarrassed?"

He shook his head. "I don't know what I was. I despised show business, but it was all I knew. Anyway, I stayed at the resort for a few months before I realized I was paying through the nose and my money would only last two years at that rate. I knew I had to do something. Then I met a guy named Joe…Joe Fontaine…who owned a construction company. He told me I could rent a house for a month for what I was paying for a week at the resort. When he offered me a job working on one of his crews, he said it was a good way to make quick money. He taught me everything I know."

Evie glanced around. "Apparently, that was a lot."

"I also rose through the ranks of his company. He told me I had an eye for budgets and knew how to get people to do things that needed to be done. By that time, I'd remodeled my first house and sold it for a bundle. I realized I could make more money flipping than I could working for somebody else. But the longer I was here, the more I realized the real money was in rentals." He opened his arms. "And here we are today."

"How'd you end up being mayor?"

He laughed. "Lots of people asked me to run, but Dotty coerced me. She said I could do a better job running the town in my spare time than most people could full time. Though she was wrong about running the town only taking my spare time, I like being connected. I like making sure things get done right. I like everyone here."

She nodded. "How'd you meet Elizabeth?"

"She was a renter." He laughed. "She hated what I had done to the apartment building she rented in. And I said something like—well, if you think you can do a better job have at it...and she rained a boatload of décor ideas down on me. And I knew she was the one."

Evie tilted her head. "Because she was sassy?"

"She wasn't sassy. My building had pushed her to her limit. Frankly, I'd never wanted to see her sassy side again."

"Ah."

Now she had her explanation for why he didn't like her, despite being attracted to her. Deep down, she was just a little too sassy for him.

She rose from her seat. "Let's clean up, and then I can be on my way."

"Really? I thought you'd want another beer."

She sat again. Or maybe she wasn't too sassy? A guy who didn't enjoy her company wouldn't ask her to stay...would he?

"I could drink another beer."

He nudged his head in the direction of the refrigerator. "Help yourself."

She pushed back her chair. "Okay."

She wondered if taking the second beer and prolonging her stay made her desperate, but she decided that was stupid. Even with no romantic relationship on the horizon, she and Pax still had to work together. And she also had no intention of abandoning Samantha. This was a step toward them getting along.

She walked to the fridge, opened it, and said, "You want another?"

"Yeah."

She turned from the fridge to find him standing by the table, paper plates in hand. "Give me two minutes to clean some of this up."

She carried the two beers into the kitchen, then returned

to the patio to bring the leftover appetizers inside to the refrigerator.

When everything was done, he glanced around. "Why don't we sit in the living room? I love those barrel chairs, but they aren't the most comfortable."

"Okay."

They took their beers into the living room, and Evie immediately noticed two things. First, he sat on the sofa with her. Second, he might have done that because he could see the door.

"Does she have a curfew?"

"She'll be home by dark."

Knowing she had to get his mind on something else, Evie said, "So how's town hall these days?"

"Not bad, but I have to admit I like splitting my time between there and Paxton Properties."

"Dotty seems like a fun person."

"You know your dad asked her out?"

She laughed. "Seriously?"

"In fairness, her ring is at the jewelers." He winced. "Your dad knew his mistake when she asked if she could bring her husband along."

"Oh, that's awful!"

"It was embarrassing for them both."

The room grew silent again. Evie looked at the big clock and saw it was only a little past eight. If she kept him company while he waited for Samantha, they'd endure almost an hour of this awkwardness.

"Tell me about Philly."

She peeked over at him. "What about Philly? My house? My job? My friends?"

"Any of it."

"Okay. My job is fun. Super fun." She paused. "Though I have to admit, I'm beginning to like doing Paradise Key's website."

"I knew it."

She grinned. "It's not what you think. I don't have designs on taking over and making it big and splashy. It's more like I go to work, chat with the other employees at Lauren's firm, read and reply to the contact emails, review the video, and then come home." She paused again. "And when I come home, I do things I don't normally do."

"Like what?"

"In Philly, I'd read a book by someone I was about to interview, or I'd go online and do a deep dive into someone's life to see if they're a candidate for the show."

"And now?"

"Now I have dinner with the girls or go for drinks. Sometimes I shop." She cast him a sidelong glance. "I do things with Sam. Fun things like get pizza."

"You're having a life."

With a rueful shrug, she turned on the sofa, putting one knee up so she was sitting sideways, facing him. "Honestly, I hate admitting this, but that's what it feels like." She snickered. "Yesterday, I took Jenna's car and drove inland to a furniture store."

"A furniture store?"

"I found myself looking around at the beach house, wondering how somebody comes up with those kinds of ideas, and I asked the girls. Sofía told me about do-it-yourself home remodeling places. Jenna told me about furniture stores. I decided to check them out."

"And?"

"The furniture store was amazing. Tons of sofas, chairs, and tables." She winced. "I mean, I knew furniture stores existed, and they had all kinds of pieces. I just never expected the impact that seeing all the stuff in one building would have on me."

His lips quirking, he faced her. "How did you decorate your house in Philly?"

"I hired a decorator."

"That's so cowardly."

She made a face. "Well, I know that now."

"What did you do at the DIY remodeling store?"

"Nothing, except realize I all but lived under a rock." She stopped and bit her lower lip. "I think that's the real conclusion I'm coming to here. As a TV star in Philly, I'm out there for everybody to see, but I'm personally protected. I don't go out much. I only socialize for charities or the show. Here, I know people. I talk to the bartenders. Go to JavaStop just to say good morning to Lorelei and hear some gossip."

"You're finding out who you are."

She tilted her head, considering. "Yeah. Sort of."

The room grew quiet again. Except this time, it wasn't uncomfortable. They were getting to know each other. And she'd just talked to him about some very personal things without worrying he'd tell anyone.

"You're so not like Lorelei."

He frowned. "What?"

"I just told you some things I hadn't even realized about myself until I said them. But I'm not worried you'll blab."

His face grew serious as if he realized the weight of what she'd said. "I'm not much on blabbing."

Her pleasure at the comment probably showed on her face, but she didn't care.

He studied her, searching for what she wasn't sure. "I think I'm going to kiss you again."

"You'd better. I don't just go on and on about private things, yet I did with you. I'm more than attracted to you, Paxton James. I like you."

"I like you, too."

His whispered admission was almost as sweet as the first press of his lips to hers.

Warm and wonderful, Paxton's kiss settled all her fears about whether he liked her. His hands drifted down her back, then up again as they nudged her closer to him, bring them together.

Every cell in her body sighed with contentment, then he

deepened the kiss, coaxing open her mouth and sending rivers of joy through her. Arousal blossomed. Her muscles relaxed.

He inched her down to the sofa, his weight settling on top of her. She lifted her arms and brushed her hands along his lean back, feeling muscles that had done practical things like knock out walls and build gardens. And she suddenly realized she liked him so much because he was real, genuine, but also smart. If he needed something, he didn't ask for it. He found a way to get it. He wasn't too proud to depend on her help with Samantha, but he also made his own way in life.

"What are we doing?"

The tickle of the words whispered against her lips almost made her laugh. Then she realized he was having second thoughts.

She should be, too. He was a serious guy, and she wanted a fling. She fully intended to return to Philadelphia—

Or so she thought.

What if she decided to stay here?

He levered himself away from her before extending his hand to help her stand.

"You're not going to say you're sorry you kissed me, are you?" She said it lightly, but she held her breath.

Pax pulled her against him. "Not this time."

He kissed her again, and her heart soared. If he asked her to stay in Paradise Key, she'd agree to it without thinking.

Just to keep this feeling. And that was wrong. She had a wonderful life in Philadelphia, a career that had meaning and purpose. She couldn't drop that for a man.

She stepped back. "I better go."

She walked to his front door, grabbed her purse from the stairway, and left without Pax saying a word to stop her. Clearly, they both had some thinking to do.

Chapter Nine

P AX JOGGED DOWN the steps the next morning to find Samantha in the kitchen, making toast.

"Hey, Dad."

His eyes narrowed. He hadn't gotten a "Hey, Dad," since January.

He strolled to the center island. "What's up?"

She shrugged. "Nothing. I was going to ask you the same thing."

He opened the cupboard, grabbed a mug, and began making himself coffee in the one-cup brewer. "I have meetings this morning. Then I need to come home and change, so I can check out the Connor place. New renters coming in. I need to make sure the cleaning service did a good job."

Sam cast him a patient look. "I was talking about Evie."

He felt his face redden. "Why would I know anything about Evie?"

She shrugged. "I don't know. She left before I got home, and I wanted to make sure she wasn't mad that I skipped out on dinner."

His coffee done, he pulled it from the brewer and took a

sip, looking at his daughter over the rim. "She wasn't mad you ran off."

Sam brightened. "So, you had a good time?"

"We had a hamburger." A thought occurred. He eased over to the island where she sat with her toast and a glass of orange juice. "You wouldn't have been matchmaking by any chance?"

She guiltily glanced at her plate. "No."

"Samantha…"

She whipped around to face him. "Would that be so bad?"

He sat on the stool beside hers. "Would it be so good?"

"Now you're making fun of me."

He sighed. "No. I phrased that wrong." Remembering that Finn's inability to talk to Evie had ruined their relationship, he said, "She's very attractive and fun to be around."

"Lots of fun to be around."

"But there's no guarantee things would work out."

"So? At least you'd be doing something and not worried about me all the time."

Ah. "Is that what this is about?"

"You hover."

He side-eyed her. "I barely talk to you."

"It feels like you're always asking where I'm going and what I did."

"Trying to make conversation." He frowned. "You know, if you'd volunteer a few things, I wouldn't have to ask."

She shook her head. "I don't want you to know everything. I want to be my own person."

As much as he wanted to tell her he wouldn't nag, would accept what she told him, if only to keep the lines of communication open, he couldn't. "The world's a dangerous place."

She rolled her eyes. "No, it's not."

"Yes, it is." He thought of the incident on Instagram the night before and added, "What happened with your friend last night...the trouble on Instagram?"

"It's a mess, but all our friends aren't like Gina Thompson, who likes to spread lies."

"People like Gina are the least of your worries. There are predators out there. Real predators, searching for innocent kids like you. If I ask where you were and who else was there, it's not to spy. It's to gauge what's going on. Your friends' parents are probably doing that, too."

"They are." She picked up her toast, but then set it down again. "It's just that you used to be so cool."

He rose and kissed the top of her head. "I'm still cool."

She sniffed a laugh. "Yeah, but you're losing it faster than you think. If I were you, I'd hang onto Evie before the male pattern baldness sets in."

He clutched his chest as if she'd shot him. "That was harsh."

"I'm just saying she's really a catch, Dad. And I like her.

I know you do, too. You just can't admit it."

"I can admit it."

Her eyes brightened. "Really?"

"Yes. But, Sam, this is just the first stages."

Her face fell. "She's going to get away! You're going to *let* her get away."

He wanted to tell her that he still thought about her mom. Not as much as he had, but he still had feelings for her. Still reached for her in the middle of the night. Still longed to talk to her some days.

But that wasn't the kind of thing a dad burdened his little girl with. Once again, he felt a connection to Finn Barclay and understood how he could have held so much back from Evie.

Little girls…no, all little kids…were supposed to be loved and protected. It was why Finn believed he was a failure. He'd tried to protect Evie, but everything he'd tried had backfired.

"You want to be treated like an adult, Sam? This is your first lesson. The one thing adults have to have more than anything else is patience. If this thing between Evie and me is supposed to work out, it will. I don't want you to do anything else like setting us up at dinner last night." Now that everything was out in the open, that set up became glaringly obvious. "Because the other thing adults know is that if you push too hard, you could ruin something that might otherwise have worked out."

Sam sighed. "I get it."

"Good. Now, I'm going to work."

He left his house and headed down the street to town hall, trying to look normal. He was getting feelings for a woman whose past was more troubled than his own. She liked his daughter. His daughter liked her.

Yet, everything inside him vibrated with something he couldn't define. Not an ache. Not sorrow. But not happiness, either. One of the most beautiful women in the world was interested in him, attracted to him, and every time his heart would leap, something odd would ripple through him and stop his happiness in its tracks.

He went into the mayor's office, grabbed the mail, and headed out again, back to Paxton Properties where he and Dotty could sort through what they would do that day.

He walked down the street as if seeing it for the first time. For years, he'd been mayor of this town and he knew every nook and cranny. But everything looked different.

A week ago, JavaStop would have reminded him of Liz. Of her baking cookies for Lorelei to sell so she could have surprise money for Christmas gifts.

Today, his head filled with thoughts of Evie's dad, sitting on the sofa longing to fix his relationship with Evie.

A week ago, a trip to a furniture store would have reminded him of time spent there with Liz. With her explaining why some pieces went together and others didn't.

Today, he longed to take Evie to his favorite furniture

gallery to see her joy over something simple and laugh with her.

He'd laughed with Liz. But not the same way he did with Evie. With Evie, everything fell together like fate. He'd fought and fought, but they still clicked.

If he were being honest, he had to face the fact that it was time to let go of Liz. Not to forget her, but to realize he needed another love. He was too young to go through the rest of his life alone.

But there was no guarantee Evie would love him. No guarantee she'd even stay in Paradise Key. She had another job, another life, twelve hundred miles away.

She might like that one better.

And that was what made him stop short. If he pursued her, he'd be building something he would most likely lose when she went back to Philly. It seemed like a foolish thing to do.

Of course, he could be thinking all this through prematurely. He and Evie needed more time together to see if what they felt really could become something. As far as Pax could tell, they had about a year.

For the first time since he met Finn Barclay, he was glad the man was something of a screw up. Because as long as his life was in the news, Evie would stay in Paradise Key.

He had to take advantage.

AFTER A MORNING of answering website emails, Evie had lunch with her friends. She and Sam texted about silly things, and then Sam mentioned the Instagram problem from the night before. Evie was about to tell her she needed to get out more—away from her phone—when she realized that might come across as preachy. If she wanted the girl away from Instagram, then she should take her away.

A little voice stopped her. What was she doing? If everything happening between her and Pax stopped, and there was a good possibility it would, Sam would get caught in the crossfire. Part of Evie absolutely wanted everything she could have with Pax, even if it was only a fling. But she did have another life—a life she loved—in Philadelphia, and she would return to it.

But how did one explain that to a twelve-year-old girl?

Actually—

Breaking up with Sam's dad to go back to her old life was a much better reason than saying she didn't love him. And she could keep Sam as a friend. Maybe have her fly to Philadelphia to spend weekends or to shop.

As situations went, moving back to Philly kept her safe and in Sam's world.

Evie packed a stack of fashion magazines in a tote and went to Sam's house.

"What we should do," Sam said as she invited Evie into the foyer, "is go for a walk." She patted her tummy. "I had a big lunch."

"Sounds good to me."

They went back to the main part of town past the bakery, JavaStop, and a boutique. Remembering her plan to bring Sam to Philly to shop, Evie said, "Let's go inside."

She opened the door and directed Samantha to enter first. Sam gasped. "So cool."

The clothes were an eclectic mix of bohemian and traditional styles, some things mixed and matched. Like a sheer, bell-sleeved paisley blouse with simple jeans.

Sam reached for a white lace tank. "I'd love this."

"It would look great with your hair."

Sam sighed. "But it's too big."

"It is now, but in another year or two, you'll be shopping here or places like this."

Sam's eyes brightened. "You think?"

"Sure. Today, we'll look around, decide what we like, and see if we can't find something close to the design in a store that caters to girls your age."

Sam nodded. After a few minutes of strolling around the sales floor, she reached for a rose-colored sundress. "There's a dance in a few weeks. Something the town holds at the end of one of our million trumped-up festivals."

Evie laughed. "It's called commerce. Your dad is smart to bring in all those things."

"I'd love to wear something like this to the dance."

Evie took it from her hand and examined it. "I don't see why we couldn't find something like this for you."

"Really?"

"Sure. Probably at the mall."

"When can we go to the mall?"

Evie chuckled. "I'm going to have to rent a car."

"Or use Dad's!"

"Okay. I'll talk to him."

"Tonight?"

Evie shook her head. "Patience."

Sam batted her eyes at Evie. "It's the perfect reason to call him. I know you like him, and I know he likes you."

Seeing the cat was out of the bag, Evie said, "Shut up! I'm not calling him. He has to call me."

Sam forked her fingers through her hair. "Oh, you adults are killing me."

Evie snickered. "Right."

They said goodbye to the proprietor and left the store.

Heading up the street, Sam said, "Want a coffee?"

Evie said, "Sure."

They ducked in to JavaStop, the bell tinkling, and stepped into the scent of fresh-brewed coffee and pastries.

"Smells like heaven." Even as Evie led Sam to the counter, a movement to her right caught her attention. She glanced over in time to see her dad.

Sam pulled money from her purse. "My treat today."

Evie should have complimented Sam on her adult behavior. Instead, she stood frozen. Her father rose from the sofa, picked up the takeout container of coffee he had setting on the low table, and headed for the door.

He didn't say hello. Didn't even acknowledge he'd seen her. But she knew he had. She'd simply told him to leave her alone so many times it appeared he was finally listening.

Sam ordered a lemonade and turned to Evie. "Um. I'll take a chai tea. Small."

Lorelei said, "Coming right up."

Evie managed to make lighthearted conversation with Sam while they sipped their drinks. She even kept things fun and interesting as they walked back to Samantha's house. But when they stepped in the door and found Pax in the kitchen putting a roast in the oven, she wanted nothing more than to collapse in his arms and weep. Not just because she and her dad were estranged, but because being with Sam, seeing how Pax was with Sam, reminded her of everything she'd missed as a child.

But there were other things, too. Pax was strong and smart, but he didn't make her feel small. They were equals. And he had become a confidante. If she wanted to weep, it wasn't just with loss. Talking to Pax about his wife, Samantha, and her dad had given Evie a sense of connection that brought understanding. Pax was helping her wrap her head around her childhood. Her life. He made her feel normal.

And she liked it—

Liked having someone who understood her. Someone she could count on.

Liked *him.*

She said a few pleasantries to Pax, realizing the feelings she was getting for him were deeper than she'd imagined. That made them dangerous. If she had a fling with someone she was falling in love with, she'd either end up hurt when she left or he'd convince her to stay.

She couldn't stay. She'd worked too hard to build her life in Philadelphia.

She turned to the door against Sam's objections.

"Stay for dinner!"

Pax frowned.

Evie said, "No, hon. I have plans with my friends tonight."

Then she blindly wandered out his door, across his porch, and to the sidewalk. Instead of going home, she went to the PR office and found an open computer where she checked for website emails to answer.

The other employees said, "Hello," and "Hey what are you doing here," until she began to feel that sense of belonging again.

She didn't mind needing a whole office full of friends.

She did mind depending on one man for her emotional security. That was a dangerous, sad place to be. At the worst time in her life, she'd had a father she should have been able to count on and he'd deserted her. She would never give another man that much control over her feelings again.

THE NEXT MORNING, dressed in a suit and tie, Pax strolled into town hall and back to his office as mayor. He knew he'd been spending a little too much time at Paxton Properties. With meetings that morning on two potential votes at the upcoming council meeting, he had some schmoozing to do.

He met with Vice-Mayor Sally Kovitz first, enjoyed a cup of coffee and a good conversation on the direction of Paradise Key. She slipped out around nine, and he made a few phone calls before his next meeting with Harold Merzdort, Council President.

Shaking Pax's hand, Harold said, "I was beginning to think we were moving town hall down the street to your Paxton Properties office."

Pax winced. "I'm buying a new condo building and seem to need to be there a little more than here lately."

Harold took a seat in front of Pax's desk. "With everything that's going on? You're giving Tyson sound bites for his campaign in the fall."

"I'm not worried."

"Maybe you should be. Tyson's begun chatting up people here in town hall, talking about how you're turning Paradise Key into its own little witness protection program."

Pax's eyes narrowed. "Witness protection program?"

"You've got two people here hiding from the press. The whole damned world knows Evie and her dad haven't spoken in ten years. Yet, you've been seen around town with them both."

He had been. But he failed to see what that had to do with anything. "Evie's helping my daughter. I've just run into Finn."

"Lorelei told Tyson that when Evie came into JavaStop the other day, her dad was out the door within seconds of seeing her."

"As you said, they don't talk."

"Lorelei said this wasn't about not talking. She said tension was so thick you could have cut it with a kite string." He leaned forward, put his elbows on his knees, and folded his hands together. "This is a fight waiting to happen. And the big worry is that some lucky reporter will figure out they are both here and fly down just in time for the fireworks."

"Trust me. Finn doesn't want to fight with his daughter."

"He told you that?"

Finn hadn't told him to keep that confidential, so Pax said, "Yes."

"What about his daughter?"

"What about her?"

"Does she want a fight?"

"She wants him gone."

Chuckling, Harold leaned back. "Well, that would certainly solve everything."

But then Finn wouldn't get his reconciliation, and something inside Pax railed at the injustice of that.

"Maybe what you need to do is have a chat with Evie.

Make her see we're teetering on the brink of becoming a fabulous tourist town and her potential fight with her dad could give us a black eye in the press."

"I don't think that's true."

Harold rose with a shrug. "You haven't been around as long as I have. You haven't seen what I've seen. The wrong word at the wrong time could ruin everything." He headed for Pax's door, but turned abruptly. "You don't have to give her a sermon. Just make sure she understands a lot is riding on her good behavior."

"Good behavior is Evie Barclay's middle name. No one was raised to be as polite and proper as she is."

Harold smiled. "Then we all have nothing to worry about."

He left Pax's office in echoing silence. Right now, Harold was his biggest supporter. But talk about Tyson could have been a subtle hint that his loyalties would sway if the situation with Evie and her dad got ugly.

He blew his breath out on a long sigh. Would it really hurt to gently remind Evie it wasn't just her reputation at stake if she had a fight with her dad on the boardwalk?

A short talk might not hurt her, but it could damage the relationship he felt building between them. He'd gotten involved with Evie because he needed help with his daughter, but she'd become the first woman to make him feel alive in years. Kissing her the other night, he'd realized he wanted her in his life as more than a casual friend and he wanted to be more than a casual friend to her.

He rose from his seat and glanced out the window. What was the saying? In for a penny, in for a pound?

He had to make a move now before advice about her dad looked like interfering. Or maybe he needed to talk to her about her dad first, then make a move, so she didn't think he'd only seduced her to make her pliable about her dad?

He was going to have to think this through before he did anything.

THE PR OFFICE kept Evie away from Pax for the next few days. But on Saturday, a tropical storm looped around to find Paradise Key. The dark sky dropped buckets of rain that created a constant drumming on the roof of the one-story bungalow. She was surprised when the sound of her doorbell penetrated the noise.

She set her book on the coffee table in front of the sofa and went to answer. A raincoat-wearing Pax stood in her doorway, dripping wet.

She scooted away from the door as she opened it wide enough for him to enter. "Come in! Oh, my gosh, what are you doing out in this?"

The only thing dire enough to bring him out in such a bad storm popped into her head. "Did something happen to my dad?" She shook her head. "No. He probably did something. Rob a liquor store maybe?"

"I do need to talk about your dad, but not because of trouble." He held up a picnic basket. "But this first." He bent and brushed a light kiss across her lips. "I missed you these past few days."

The relief that washed through her almost made her faint. She might not want to depend on him for emotional security, but the way he so casually kissed her filled her with pleasure. And she'd already figured out how to explain a fling to Sam. There was nothing wrong with them being together. Nothing at all.

She took the picnic basket from him. "I could use some fun."

"You absolutely look like you could use some fun." He shrugged out of the raincoat, hanging it on one of the three hooks by the door. For the first time, she noticed the small rubber mat beneath it as it caught the rain dripping from his coat.

She laughed. "It seems the landlord thought of everything."

He bent and pressed another quick kiss on her lips. "He always does."

Her heart shimmied. The kisses had been brief and fun, and should have been meaningless, but now that she knew Pax a little better, she recognized he didn't do anything without a purpose.

He'd meant those wonderful kisses. Brief. Light. Happy.

He was happy.

Happy to see her.

He took the picnic basket from her and set it on the coffee table, then flipped a switch on the wall. Flames leapt in the fireplace.

"Oh."

"See why this is the perfect day for a picnic?"

"Yes." Warmth seeped into the room. Her silly heart expanded as she got into the mood. He was happy. She was happy.

He pulled a bottle of wine out of the basket, and she headed for the kitchen. "I have glasses."

"Tsk-tsk. Glasses? This is a picnic." He retrieved two red Solo cups before twisting the lid off the bottle.

"You bought wine that doesn't have a cork?"

He shrugged. "Picnic, remember?"

She laughed.

"I'll bet you've never been on a picnic where you didn't have a cork screw."

"I have this little one that fits into my purse."

He stopped her explanation with a kiss. This one was slow and deep. All the tension drained from Evie's body in a long wave. The rain drummed on the roof while the warmth of the fire surrounded them. But all she could think about was Pax. His body pressed against hers. The way he kissed her. Not quick and fun like his first kisses. But with an emotion that took them to a new level. He liked her. He wasn't afraid to say it now.

He broke the kiss. Dazed and a little awestruck, she stood by the coffee table, watching as he reached for the blanket she'd been under while reading. He whipped it off the sofa, the quick move billowing it open, then spread it on the floor in front of the fireplace.

He poured wine into the Solo cups, then pulled two sandwiches from the basket before he sat in front of the fire.

She stared at him.

"Aren't you hungry?"

She was starving, but not for food. For the feeling that had coursed through her when he'd kissed her. She'd never experienced it before. Not in a one-night stand or a long-term relationship. The lure of it drew her to the fire—to him.

But he motioned to the blanket. When she was settled on it, he handed her a sandwich. She pulled it from the plastic bag as he got up and turned the fire down to a whisper of warmth.

He grinned. "Now that I'm out of the wet raincoat and all warmed up, we don't need the heat, just the ambiance."

Some of the richest, smartest men in the world had tried to seduce her with things like champagne and yachts. This guy gave her a sandwich and a fire—in Florida, in the summer.

She bit into her sandwich and shook her head with amusement.

He leaned in a brushed his thumb across the corner of her mouth. "You had a crumb."

His touch on her now-sensitive lips sent a crackle of electricity through her.

The corner of his mouth lifted as he took in the dumbfounded expression on her face. "I don't just think you need a little fun today. I think you have to change your entire definition of fun. Because what I've been seeing is that you know how to entertain everybody but yourself." His smile grew. "Tomorrow, we're going to Home Depot."

The absurdity of it made her snort. "You know, one minute it seems like you're seducing me. The next, you're taking me to Home Depot." She met his gaze. "Are you confused?"

"For the first time in a long time, I know exactly what I want."

The heat in his eyes surpassed the heat coming out of the fireplace, and she swallowed.

He leaned in and covered her mouth with his before pulling back. "But the problem with intimacy is that people confuse it with sex." At her raised eyebrow, he smirked. "Oh, sex is definitely part of it. But so are a lot of other things. If you can't come with me to Home Depot, then you really don't understand me. And if I can't tell when you need something special..." He shrugged. "Then maybe I'm not paying enough attention."

He captured her mouth again, running his hands down

her arms as he scooted closer on the blanket. She tossed her sandwich to the coffee table, burrowing into him.

He deepened the kiss, coaxing her mouth open, as his hand roamed to her breast. She sighed with a combination of contentment and need. When his hand drifted to the snap on her jeans, she pulled him down to the blanket.

Chapter Ten

A N HOUR LATER, when Pax realized they were about to make love for the second time, he lifted Evie from the blanket and carried her into the bedroom. Ambiance was one thing. Hardwood floors were quite another.

Afterward, spent, but content, he rolled to his side and pulled Evie with him. "This has always been one of my favorite bedrooms."

She sat up halfway, so she could look down on him. "Is that what you do? Rent to single women and then seduce them in the bedroom to see if you like it?"

His laughter filled the room. "Wow. Suspicious."

She drew in a breath and squeezed her eyes shut. "It's my big fault. Started with my dad and moved into every relationship I've ever had. I'd say I'm sorry, but it's such a part of me now that I'll understand if it makes you want to run screaming."

"After what we just did?" He ran a hand over her bare breast with an appreciative noise. "It'll take more than a little suspicion to make me run screaming."

She lay down again, resting her head on his shoulder. "You're a brave man."

"I like to think so."

She shook her head, and he loved the feeling of her hair shuffling back and forth against his shoulder. He'd also loved her surrender. Not with fear or resignation that they had to do something about their attraction, but with total and complete honesty.

She was vulnerable. But so was he.

"And I don't sleep around."

She nodded. "No mayor worth his salt would risk the scandal."

He peered at her. "Do you think of everything in terms of reputation? Appearances?"

"It's the way I was brought up."

He thought of Harold and his fear that Evie or her father would cause a scandal, and he suddenly realized how ridiculous that was. She'd do anything to avoid a confrontation.

Still, Harold wanted him to talk to her, so he would. Not for Harold, but to be the one to bring it up to her so she didn't hear it from Tyson or Harold and be embarrassed.

"Some people on the council are worried you or your dad might cause a scandal that could ruin all the progress we've made turning Paradise Key into an elite tourist destination."

She sat up, pulling the sheet with her. "Really? The very fact that my father and I are here turns it into an elite tourist destination."

He burst out laughing. "Well, that's certainly a good way

of looking at things."

"As long as we don't fight and end up on YouTube."

"Actually, we'd rather you didn't fight. Then it would be okay for you and your dad to end up on YouTube."

"Sure. Show the world celebrities are safe here."

"Now that's a tagline Lauren could probably put to good use."

She giggled and snuggled back against him. "Not on your life. There's no way in hell I want to end up on YouTube, and I'll bet my father doesn't either."

He said, "Hmmm." He'd spent his life around the rich and famous. Or so he'd thought. Evie and her dad, albeit that he was broke, were a whole different level of celebrity. While his mom would have loved to have someone video her and put it on YouTube, Evie and her dad meticulously avoided that kind of publicity.

They wanted to live real lives without fear that somebody would exploit them.

That really was the kind of tourist they wanted to attract. Big money people wanting to keep a low profile, even as they interacted with the locals.

Actually, now that he thought about it, that was what Evie wanted. A place to be normal. Not hiding when things went wrong and only going out when things were good. But engaging with her neighbors no matter what her circumstances because as small towns went, this one might gossip but they could also be fiercely protective. She'd been here long enough that the residents, even Lorelei, would protect her from outsiders.

But he bet she didn't know that.

"We should put on raincoats and run to JavaStop to get a cup of coffee."

"We have perfectly good wine in the living room."

He rolled over until he was halfway on top of her and could gaze into her luminous gray eyes. "Yeah, but we could make a spectacle of ourselves, have everybody see us together looking like a couple and start the gossip mill running."

Her eyes widened. "Are you nuts?"

"No. I'm trying to show you that we can do what we want. People here can and will gossip, but you're still safe with us."

She blinked.

"What did you do in Philly? How'd you get everybody to let you alone?"

"No one leaves me alone. I combatted my reputation by proving myself as a reporter and talk-show host, but I stay in my house most of the time."

The picture of her life began to form. She'd never had a discussion with her dad about her mom dying, about him stealing from her, or about her grief. She'd locked it away, found a life that she could control, and never dealt with any of it. "Sounds hard."

She combed her fingers through her hair. "It is what it is."

"And I say it doesn't have to be." He jumped out of bed. Held out his hand. "Come on. Let's go make some gossip so we get it over with, people can accept us, and we can have fun."

"That's ridiculous!"

"No, it isn't. It's getting out ahead of it. It's showing people we will be who we are. It's saying go ahead and gossip. We don't care." He tugged on her arm to urge her out of bed. "This is how you handle your reputation and still have a life. You give people the story, on your terms, and let them gossip if they like."

Her look of confusion shifted until her eyes shone and her lips curled upward. "It sounds crazy."

"If nothing else, it will be fun."

"I'll give your theory a whirl."

"It's not a theory. It's what I do. How I've stayed mayor in a small town despite gossip, back biting, and craziness."

"Okay, then." She rolled out of bed. Gloriously naked. Wonderfully his—

But for how long?

He told his brain to shut up. Reminded himself that he had a plan. Then caught her hand and led her into the living room where they redressed.

"I did like that red bra, by the way."

She laughed. "You're crazy."

"And sometimes, I think you're too sane."

She bobbed her head, considering that. "Maybe."

"This trip to the coffee shop will change that. You're going to see how much fun it is to be yourself and not give a damn."

She didn't have a raincoat, so he let her wear his. It was another sign they were "together." Under the big black umbrella that they found in a back closet, they raced to JavaStop, laughing like two kids.

When they stepped inside, he stole a kiss just to make sure Lorelei got the story in one quick action.

As they approached the counter hand in hand, Lorelei stared at them.

"Today's a day for coffee," he told her as she took them in with astonished eyes. "Though I think Evie's more of a tea drinker."

"I am."

Lorelei still stared.

"So, one coffee. One tea. And this brownie."

Lorelei blinked. "Brownie?"

"Yes."

"You only eat brownies when you've trounced Tyson in a meeting."

"Because I'm happy." He smiled at Evie. "I'm happy today."

Lorelei's look of confusion became a big grin. "One brownie it is."

"Make it two," Evie said. "We had perfectly good sandwiches back home, but he hauled me out here before I could finish mine."

They settled in on the sofa with their brownies and warm drinks. When someone came in, Pax waved and watched their reactions. But mostly, he watched Evie.

She'd never dealt with her past, only found ways to tolerate it. She worked hard to keep a good reputation, and only had surface relationships. Even her best friends lived twelve hundred miles away, so she could keep her secrets.

But he didn't do surface relationships. That was how potentially wonderful connections fizzled.

He didn't believe in secrets. They caused people to lie.

If he wanted this, and he did, he was going to have to help her out of her shell, her prison.

And the only way he could do that would be to help her handle the situation with her dad. But he wouldn't go into that hornet's nest without all the information ...which meant he was going to have to investigate Finn.

ONE MINUTE, EVIE was walking on air. The next, she was totally confused. Pax had told her that Sam was on a weekend trip to Disney World with a friend and her parents. So, he could stay the night Saturday. He made her breakfast on Sunday morning. But after the pancakes were eaten, he was packed and gone.

He hadn't exactly behaved like the Blues Brothers on a

mission, but there was something on his mind.

A few minutes after he was out the door, Jenna called. "I heard from at least three sources that you were at JavaStop with Pax on Saturday, and Lorelei said you were cozy."

She laughed at the antiquated phrasing, just as there was a knock at her door. "We *were* cozy." As Pax had said, there was no sense denying it. It was better to get out ahead of the story and control it.

But she'd have told Jenna the truth even if Pax had made her promise not to tell anyone. Her friends weren't "anyone." They were the people with whom she was the most honest. Still, after her weekend with Pax, she was beginning to realize she held a lot back from them, too.

She started toward the door. "He brought a picnic on Saturday. Turned on the fireplace. What woman could resist that?"

It sounded so easy when she said it like that. Fireplace. Picnic. Seduction. And with that explanation, her friends would see how she could succumb. But so much more had happened in those very short twenty hours. He'd seduced her, but with emotion. Not just sex. Then eased her out of bed and into the world to announce they were a couple. No press release. No drip campaign so people could get adjusted.

Nope. He just took her hand and announced to the world they were together.

It was the most confusing thing.

Jenna said, "I want details," as Evie opened the door and

found Sofía, bag of donuts in hand.

"Whoever you are on the phone with," Sofía said, "hang up. You and I need to talk."

Lauren came rushing up the walk. She stopped by Sofía. "Me too."

"Jenna's on the phone."

Jenna said, "What? Who is that?"

Evie took a long breath. "It's Sofía and Lauren. Sofie has donuts. I've got a coffeemaker. So just bring yourself." She hung up the phone.

Coming inside, Lauren said, "Since when do you let yourself become the object of gossip?"

Since Pax had lured her into it, held out his hand, and told her everything would be okay.

But could she admit that to her friends, admit she was that smitten, or he was that wonderful? What if this relationship failed? Worse, what if she fell in love and he didn't?

This had potential embarrassment, not to mention heartache, written all over it.

Pretending nonchalance she didn't feel, Evie shrugged. "It's a small town. How far can it go?"

"All it takes is one tourist with a camera for this to get back to Philly."

She knew that. But everything Pax had said came tumbling back. *Face it head-on. Face it realistically.* "So? Pax is gorgeous. My audience will probably applaud my taste in men."

Sofía laughed, but Lauren shook her head. "I know how much your reputation means to you. It might be okay to be silly here, but hosts in big cities don't flaunt their love lives."

The thought of losing the good reputation she had in Philly tightened Evie's chest and gave her a vaguely sick feeling in her stomach, but her front door opened. Jenna raced in.

"I don't care what anybody else has said. I think Pax is a wonderful guy."

And that was when it hit her. The reason she had the vague sense of unease. It wasn't her reputation she was worried about. It was perception. She and Pax might be having a fling, but everybody else saw this as permanent.

Evie held up her hands for everybody to stop. "Let's all get a grip here. I slept with the guy—"

"You slept with him?" Sofía gasped.

Lauren said, "We thought you'd just gotten coffee."

Evie headed to the coffeemaker, needing a minute.

Jenna said, "He pulled the fireplace-in-a-rainstorm move."

Sofía sighed. "Oh. So romantic."

It had been romantic, and Evie had been unprepared for it. More than that, she hadn't been prepared for the emotion of it. For the feeling there was another person in the world who understood her and hadn't bolted, but wanted to be part of her life.

Her stomach rolled. There was that feeling of permanency again.

She didn't trust it. Never had. Never would.

Nothing in her life had been permanent. She'd lost her mom before she'd really had a chance to get to know her, the grandfather she'd loved, the home that had been safe and happy, the father she'd always believed loved her.

She should be content with a fling.

She *was* content with a fling.

It was all she wanted.

Now she just had to convince Pax of that.

She got four mugs from Pax's well-stocked cupboards. "Sofía, open those donuts."

SITTING AT HIS computer on Sunday afternoon, Pax flicked through news stories from the years after Evie's mom died, but he wasn't getting very far with his investigation of Finn Barclay. He had an account from Evie's dad that didn't put him in the best light, and for that reason alone, Pax was tempted to believe him—except he'd also been raised by an actress. He'd watched his mom shift from sexy starlet to homespun mom in seconds, depending on what the director, producer, or casting agency told her they wanted to see. She was even faster at switching personas with reporters.

Finn had been a much more successful actor than Pax's mom. It was quite possible he was acting when he'd told Pax how sorry he was for his past with Evie, trying to get Evie on his side. Or, more appropriately, trying to get Pax on his side, hoping Pax would sway Evie.

And Finn had a very good motive. If he really was broke, he'd need Evie's money for his defense team to fight the charges against him.

The thought that Finn might use him to get Evie to cover his legal fees made the hair on the back of Pax's neck stand on end. That was a better motivation for him being in Paradise Key than the hope of reconciling with his daughter.

Still, Pax's troubles with Samantha were coming upon him like a storm, so he also realized how easy it could have been for Finn to screw up with Evie and not know how to get himself back on track.

With all that swirling around in his head, Pax sat at the computer in his home office for an entire day, reading the accounts of the plane crash that had killed Evie's grandfather and mom. He looked for anything that might have been written on Finn's financial troubles, his gambling, anything that might corroborate his story, but found virtually nothing. All this happened long before social media, and the people who were social media now didn't know Finn or care to post about him.

Tired after a long day of staring at a computer screen, Pax rubbed his hands across his eyes. He didn't know Finn's friends, and even if he did, this wasn't something he'd talk about with strangers. If he had been in the little town in

Connecticut that Finn had called home in his bad years, Pax would simply go from bar to bar until he found a bartender who remembered Finn. But he wasn't. He was in Florida, over a thousand miles away.

Still, he did have one potential source. His former agent. He wasn't wild about contacting her, but he would—to protect Evie.

He reached for his cell phone and began scrolling through the contacts. The entertainment industry was a very small world. Finn might not have had a part in over twenty years, but at the time of his troubles, he'd taken a few roles. If there was one thing Pax had learned from his mom, it was that agents knew everything.

He found three numbers for Maureen. He bypassed her office, placing the call to a private line.

She answered on the first ring. "Well hello, handsome."

"Hey, Maureen."

"I knew it was only a matter of time before you wanted back in the game."

He laughed. "Nope. Don't want back in the game. I'm actually the mayor of a small town."

"So was Sonny Bono. Didn't stop him from taking cameos and walk-ons."

"I'm quite happy."

She sighed. "Too bad. With a face like yours, you could have made a mint."

"I doubt it since I wasn't much of an actor. Listen, I've

got a little problem and need some information."

"What kind of information?"

"First, you have to take a vow of silence."

Her laugh was punctuated by the flick of her lighter, then the sound of her breath streaming to release cigarette smoke. "A vow of silence?"

"I know where Finn Barclay is."

"Holy crap! He's in your town, isn't he?" He could picture Maureen coming to attention in her seat. "Get me three pictures and I could get top dollar for you from a tabloid."

"No."

She sighed.

"Vow of silence."

"Damn my curiosity. But if a vow of silence is the only way I get to hear the dirt first, then you have my word. I won't discuss this with anyone."

"I need to know about his past."

"His past? Are you afraid he's going to steal the parking meters?"

He considered that. "Not precisely the parking meters, but there's some stuff at stake."

"You know he stole from his daughter's trust fund."

"Yes."

"The man was a booze hound."

"Reformable?"

"In this town, I've seen the worst alcoholics turn into saints. Everybody's capable of being reformed."

"Rumor has it he sold his house."

"*Lost* his house." The cigarette lighter flicked again. "To be honest, now that I'm remembering him, the story is sort of pathetic. He adored his wife and when he lost her he spiraled. Fell into a bottle and never came out."

"He claims he gambled."

"He could have. But the real bottom line is he just couldn't get over his wife's death. He could have had any woman in Hollywood, but he wanted the princess. Pissed her dad off royally. But they made a good couple. And Finn pulled his weight while she was alive. He didn't exactly make blockbusters. He made movies that paid him consistently— I'd imagine he did that to be able to support his wife in the manner to which she'd become accustomed."

"He lost touch with his daughter."

"Doesn't surprise me. He kept up a façade in LA that he was still a big man...you know, throwing money around trying to scrounge up work. But the thing about keeping up a façade is that you either have to be good with details or you have to avoid conversations."

"He tells me he avoided conversations with his daughter."

"Add stealing from her trust fund to that, and the kid had no reason to like or trust him."

"That's what he thinks."

Maureen sighed. "Are you sure you won't get me a picture? Just one..."

He laughed. "No. My town is a happy little haven. We want to keep it that way."

"Too bad."

He hung up the phone feeling a lot better. He didn't like the idea that Finn had been a bad father, but he wasn't drinking anymore, and he wanted to fix his relationship with Evie. He was on the right track. And whether Evie knew it or not, she needed him. Or maybe she simply needed to understand to be able to get on with her life.

That left Pax with one of two options. Simply wait for the topic of her dad to come up in conversation and then tell her the things her father had told him.

Or start the conversation and hope she didn't think he was a traitor for talking to her dad and confirming Finn's story.

Chapter Eleven

Tuesday morning, the storm was only a distant memory as sun poured down on the boardwalk. Evie watched as Pax made his way around the side of the resort with Sam racing ahead of him.

"Hey!"

"Hey!" Sam's dark lashes held just a hint of mascara. Instead of lipstick, she wore only a little gloss. "I see you're getting really good with enhancing what you have while keeping the makeup less obvious."

"It's not hard," Sam said. "You just have to remember what enhance means." She grinned. "But the second I turn thirteen, I'm trying eyeliner."

Evie laughed. Instead of stopping on the boardwalk and preparing for his shoot, Pax headed toward her with a determined expression. He caught her hands and pulled her in for a quick kiss on the lips.

Dave's eyebrows rose. Sam's head about snapped off her neck when she twisted it around to see.

Pax said, "Good morning," then turned toward the boardwalk. "Let's get this party started."

Dave hit a few buttons before raising his hand for the

countdown. "Five, four, three, two, one..."

He pointed at Pax, who grinned. "Hey, y'all. June is turning out to be a fantastic month here in Paradise Key, Florida. We had a little storm over the weekend, but if you're smart, you make good use of a fireplace and a nice bottle of red."

Evie felt her cheeks redden. She slid a sidelong glance at Sam, who side-eyed her. Sam had already figured out that there was something going on between Evie and her dad. But Sam was in the beginning stages of understanding relationships, so Evie doubted she had guessed—or God forbid Pax had told her—that they'd slept together.

Still, the situation was a nail biter.

What if Sam asked?

Was it Evie's place to tell the girl she'd slept with her father?

Evie stifled the urge to cover her face with her hands and groan.

"This week, Paradise Key hosts our famous chicken pot pie cook off. The fire company will be doing a barrel fight—"

Evie called, "Cut."

Instead of scowling, Pax smiled. "What?"

"You might call it a barrel fight, but it's really a barrel-roll competition."

His dimples popped. When his green eyes locked with hers, the warm, syrupy feelings of lying beside him listening to the drumming rain came back, filling her chest with warmth and happiness.

"Okay. Got it. Barrel-roll competition."

Dave did the countdown, Pax started from the beginning. When he got to the barrel roll, he said, "The fire company will be doing a barrel-roll competition. Votes cost a dollar, and all proceeds go to the fire company that wins. Wear a T-shirt and flip-flops and get in on the fun."

Evie said, "Cut!"

That interruption seemed to bring him up short, but he said, "What?"

"How do people get in on the fun? Why T-shirts and flip-flops?"

Pax patiently said, "Because they are going to get wet. When you stand a few feet away from two fire companies using hoses to move a barrel, water's going to fly."

"You're going to have to get that in there somehow."

From the expression on Pax's face, it was clear his patience had begun to thin. "You don't think they're smart enough to know they'll get wet standing by dueling fire hoses?"

She shrugged. "I had to look it up."

He sighed, walked back to his beginning spot, and started over. This time when he got to the barrel-roll competition, he did a quick, cute explanation that made her heart pitter-patter so much that when he leaned in and got personal with the audience, she didn't care. He was adorable. Not in a goofy way, but in that gorgeously sexy, carefree

Southern guy way that made her breathing stutter.

"Now I'm going to be serious for a second because this is really important. If you like parasailing, you're going to want to be with us the week after next. I'm telling you now so you have a chance to get hotel reservations. We have four parasailing companies coming to town to give demonstrations and free five-minute rides."

He leaned in even closer. "I know the companies are hoping that five minutes of breezing over the ocean will whet your appetite and you'll want a longer ride, but, hey, everybody's got to make a living, right?"

He finished with a quick, "So come on down to Paradise Key, Florida. We'll be waiting for you."

"And cut."

That was Dave. Evie had been gazing at Pax, her heart pounding in her chest, her mouth dry. He wasn't just sexy. He had a personality that wrapped around her and made her feel connected to him.

She wasn't just falling in love with him. He was pulling her into his orbit, making her part of his life.

Worse, she loved the feeling. She loved it so much she was beginning to worry about having a fling with him. He wasn't the kind of guy who could keep things casual…but she also had to admit what she felt was stronger and deeper than anything she'd ever felt. And a new question, a question she'd never dealt with, arose—

What would *she* do when this was over?

How would she handle the broken heart that was sure to be worse than anything she'd ever known?

"Are you coming to the house tonight?"

Sam's question knocked her out of her thoughts.

"I don't know."

"You have to come," Pax said as he approached them. "I'm making jambalaya."

And there it was. The sweet Southern accent. The lure of food. The tug of time with him. Him and Sam...like a family. The family she'd never had.

Fear spiked. Memories of her dad becoming a stranger inch by inch filled her, along with the knowledge that if she let her relationship with Pax go any further, she was going to get hurt. Really hurt. And so were Pax and Sam. There could be no fling with Pax. The man threw himself into everything. She had to stop this now.

"I...um...can't tonight."

Pax caught her gaze and forced her attention to him. "Seriously?"

She nervously glanced away. "Yeah. I'm doing something with the girls."

"Something, huh?"

Oh, God, nerves had made her unable to lie and he'd caught her in the half-truth.

But her fear of getting involved, putting her whole heart and soul into him and then losing him, was stronger than her desire to look like a good person in his eyes.

She said, "Yeah. We'll figure out what we're doing to-night when they get to my house." Then she turned to Dave. "Ready?"

He said, "Yeah," and, camera in hand, followed her.

AT SIX O'CLOCK that night, she made herself a pitcher of lemonade and carried it, a glass of ice, and her book out to the deck. She set everything on the small table by the chaise lounge and got comfortable.

She hadn't read two pages before Pax appeared at the top of the steps leading from the white sand of the beach to her deck.

"So that's how you spend an evening out with the girls?"

Embarrassment caught her in an ugly grip, but she re-fused to be upset about protecting herself.

"I didn't think it was a good idea for me to see you and Sam tonight."

"I had every intention of shipping Sam to a friend's house."

Trapped in the spell of his sexy voice and desire-filled eyes, she almost dropped the book.

"I think you and I need some more you and me time."

"Why? So I can fall in love with you?"

His eyes sparked with amusement. "That's the goal, yes. But there are hundreds of stages in between."

She lifted her chin. "What if I don't want to fall?"

"Then we'll have a hell of a good time while it lasts."

"And then I'll be the scarlet woman who slept with the mayor and then dumped him."

"Who says I'm not going to dump you?"

"Actually, that's the bigger worry."

He walked over to the chaise, then stooped beside it so they were eye level. "Do I look like the kind of guy who goes around looking for women's hearts to break?"

"I don't know. I've really only dated accountants and lawyers, and I broke two of their hearts."

He shook his head with a quiet chuckle. "There. See? We're getting to know each other. That's what this time together is supposed to be about."

She bit her lip, gazing at him.

He caught her hand and pulled her from the chaise. "Come on. Let's walk on the beach. Or flip through your playlist so I can tell what kind of person you are by what you listen to."

She pushed a playful hand at him, but the second she was standing, he bent and brushed his lips across hers. "Hi."

Her heart stuttered. How could such a simple word be infused with so much intimacy? "Hi."

"I missed you."

She swept her gaze over him. His perfect green eyes, handsome face, the black five o'clock shadow dusting his chin and cheeks. "You just saw me this morning."

"And you yelled at me again."

"I didn't yell. I was making sure the video was the best it could be."

He sighed.

"Oh, now, don't pout." Something about the way he got insulted over her direction of the video appealed to her. Making that video was the only time she felt in control with him. "I'm not going to let a sloppy video go online. They are important."

"You're not going to talk about the click-to-reservation rate, are you? Because if you are, I'm taking a nap."

With a quick head shake, she said, "Now where's that Southern charm you like to sprinkle like sugar?"

He laughed. "It does come in handy." He looped his arms around her waist. "But I use it sparingly with you. It's nice to be able to be myself with someone."

It was nice for her, too. The biggest part of the reason she liked being around him was that he let her be herself. No pretending her past didn't exist or didn't matter. No pretense.

He nibbled at her lips, asking to be let in, and she opened for him, getting lost in the kiss. The sounds of the ocean mixed and mingled with the salty air and warm sun, and her thoughts drifted away.

His hands cruised her back. Her arms went around his neck, so her fingers could slide through his silky black hair.

"What do you say we delay the walk on the beach?"

She pulled away slightly to look into his eyes. "You've got something in mind?"

"Yeah, I do. But it requires we go into your bedroom and get rid of some clothes."

Totally seduced by the moment, she told herself to forget the future and forget her worries. After catching his hand, she led him inside.

"WHAT ARE YOU doing tomorrow?"

Taking the sheet with her, Evie sat up, amazed he could go from breathtaking sex to mundane conversation. "I'll be in the PR office in the morning. Maybe do something with Sam in the afternoon."

"She likes you. A lot."

Now that the crazy needs he inspired had been satisfied, her worries came back full force. "And we're going to have to make sure she isn't hurt because of what we're going."

His face scrunched. "Dating?"

She motioned around her rumpled bed. "This is hardly dating."

"Then you're not doing it right."

A snort of amusement escaped. "You Southerners. Think you know it all."

"We do. It's my theory that it all stems from the days before air conditioning. There wasn't a lot anybody could do in the hot sun, so we learned to just enjoy an afternoon."

"Such a load of bull."

"I am a politician."

She grinned. "And I am hungry for pancakes."

"Really?"

"Yes. I can make them just like my mom's."

"Apple, right?"

She nodded.

He slapped her butt. "So what are we waiting for?"

He pulled on his jeans, and she slid into a silky robe. She tied the sash and headed for the kitchen.

"The trick is apple juice."

When they reached the living room, he tossed his T-shirt on the back of the sofa before walking to the center island and taking a seat. "Ah."

"I'm serious." She reached into the cupboard and pulled out a box of pancake mix. "Replace water with apple juice in the mix, and you have apple pancakes."

"You're cheating. You're using a mix."

"I didn't learn how to cook until I was twenty, in my own apartment on campus. Be glad I can use a mix."

HE DECIDED SHE was probably right, but also realized that her using her mom's trick for apple pancakes was a very good way to get her talking about her childhood.

He wasn't sure how much he'd spill of what he knew about her dad's troubles or if he'd even find an opportunity to wedge in anything at all. But this was a good first step. Only an idiot wouldn't realize that most of Evie's hesitancy about relationships came from the back-to-back losses she'd suffered when her mom and grandfather died, and her dad pulled away from her. He was pretty sure she'd adjusted to the capricious way life stole her mom and grandfather. Now he had to help her accept some of what had happened later to get her to trust again.

Because if he couldn't get her to trust, it wouldn't matter how good they were in bed, how happy they made each other, she would never stay.

"Tell me more about growing up with a famous mom and dad."

She pulled out a bowl and measuring cup, then poured in the pancake mix. "My parents weren't the famous ones. My grandfather was. The man couldn't go anywhere without getting mobbed." She measured the apple juice. "He was grouchy, surly, and frequently shook his cane at reporters or people who would come up to our table in a restaurant, asking for stock tips."

"Shook his cane, huh?" No wonder Finn had been afraid of him.

"Then we'd get in the limo and he'd do an imitation of himself being grouchy, shaking the cane, and he'd laugh and laugh because he wasn't grouchy at all. He was the nicest guy in the world. I'd say, 'One of these days, somebody's going to find out you're an old softie.' And he'd laugh and say there were too many people who'd seen him being mean for anyone to believe it."

She stopped and sighed. "I miss him. I often wonder what my life would have been like if they hadn't died. He and my mom." She twisted her lips. "My dad used to be so happy."

Pax very carefully said, "I actually spoke to my agent the other day."

She frowned, obviously confused by what seemed like a change of subject. "You did?"

"Yeah, she asked me if I wanted to get back into show biz and I told her no." It wasn't really a lie. At one point in the conversation, she had asked him.

Evie rolled her eyes.

"But we got to talking about your dad—because after I made her take a vow of silence, I told her he was here." Having stretched the truth once, he would not stretch it again. From here on out, total honesty. "Anyway, she remembered how much he loved your mom."

"Oh, he did," Evie said without a second of hesitancy. "Our house was filled with so much love and laughter." She whipped the apple juice into the pancake mix. "I think that's part of why I missed it so much when it was gone."

"I'll bet."

There was his intro. The way to explain some things

about her father, his troubles, why their relationship had fallen apart. And how the extenuating circumstances shouldn't color how she felt about all relationships.

The doorbell rang, and Pax about jumped out of his seat. "You really did have the girls coming tonight?"

"No." She winced. "Little white lie."

He nodded. Not sure what to make of that, except he knew she was struggling with their relationship and avoiding him was the way she'd decided to protect herself.

"I'll get it then, since you're in a robe."

She batted a hand. "No. It can only be one of the girls. No one else visits." She dried her hands on a dish towel. "I'll be right back."

With the open-floorplan, he could see his daughter when Evie opened the door.

"Sam?"

He watched Sam's eyes widen as they took in Evie's silky robe before they bounced over to him, sitting without a shirt at the kitchen island.

"Dad?"

He jumped off his seat. "Samantha." Striding to the door, via the sofa so he could grab his shirt and pull it over his head, he said, "What's up? I thought you were at Amanda Taylor's."

"Her dad burned himself on the grill. Her mom took him to the hospital." She looked from Evie to him again. "I...I thought you'd be here."

Pax about melted into nothing on the hardwood floors when Sam spun away from the door. "You know what? I'll just go home."

Chapter Twelve

BEFORE HE HAD a chance to reach her, Sam raced off down the beach. He pressed a quick kiss to Evie's mouth. "I've got to go after her."

She tightened the sash on her robe. "I'm sorry."

He brushed his lips reassuringly over hers. "Don't be sorry! This is more my fault than yours. It's also something she's going to have to get used to."

He sprinted after Samantha, but she was quick. By the time they got to the street, he realized she was going home and decided to give her the ten minutes of privacy it would take to reach the house.

Once she was inside, he gave her another minute before he followed. "Samantha!"

"In the kitchen, Dad."

He made his way to her. "Did you have supper?"

"Amanda's dad burnt himself trying to make supper, remember?" She opened the refrigerator, then took out some bread and deli meat.

"Right. Got it." He glanced around. "Evie was making pancakes."

Her face reddened. "You can go back."

He tapped the tip of her nose. "Nope. I think you and I need to have a conversation."

She sighed. "I already know about sex."

Pax winced. "I remember that short clumsy talk." It had been the low point of his life.

"I've learned a lot more since then."

Which was what worried him and was why, for the love of all that was holy, he couldn't let the lines of communication close between them.

"Did you find out about the part where people are supposed to love and respect each other?"

She groaned.

"Look, Sam. Our lives aren't going work if you decide to shut me out."

"I don't want to talk about sex with you."

"Do you think I want to talk about sex with you?"

It took a second of confusion, but she eventually laughed. "Maybe not."

He slid onto a stool and faced her. "Here's the thing. Evie and her dad were a lot like us."

Sam frowned. "Her mom died?"

"Yes. But her dad didn't even try to keep them talking. He sent Evie to boarding school and when she came home for visits, he had trouble talking to her."

"Because he didn't know her anymore."

"That and the fact that they had some financial problems."

"I thought Evie was rich."

"She is. When her mom and grandfather were killed in a plane crash, Evie inherited all her grandfather's money."

"Oh."

"Her dad tried to keep up the image that everything was fine, but it wasn't. He was broke."

Sam slid onto the stool beside him.

"I know some of this is a bit over your head and maybe seems irrelevant, but my point is that because Finn didn't talk to Evie, they grew apart. They haven't spoken beyond a yelling match they had in my office a few weeks ago. It's been ten years." He sucked in a breath. "I don't want that to happen to us."

She met his gaze with big brown eyes so much like Elizabeth's that his heart hurt. "I don't want that either."

"Then we have to work at this. Talk when you'd rather storm away."

She groaned.

"Hey, I went after you when I didn't want to talk to you about my relationship with Evie. But I did it because you have a right to know what's going on, and I'm not a coward."

She giggled.

"I'm not. Believe it or not, facing you is sometimes the hardest thing I do all day."

"I'm scarier than Tyson?"

He ruffled her hair. "Everyone's scarier than Tyson." He

rose from the stool. "Wanna go get a pizza?"

She stood, gathered up the sandwich ingredients, and put them back. "Should we ask Evie?"

"No. She'd probably rather not join in on tonight's festivities. We'll give her a day or two to get her equilibrium."

Sam nodded. "Then we'll have her over for dinner tomorrow or Thursday."

"Thursday should be just the right amount of time."

"Good because I found a video I want to ask her about."

He directed her to the front door. "Good."

She paused and turned to look at him. "I do love you, Dad."

His heart rattled in his chest. For a few seconds, he didn't think he'd be able to speak. "I love you, too."

She opened the door. "Let's go get our pizza."

They strolled down the two blocks to get to the pizza shop. And the whole time, Pax kept thinking that Finn Barclay would probably love to hear those five simple words from his daughter.

WEDNESDAY NIGHT, EVIE really did make plans with her friends. It had taken her a restless Tuesday night to realize she was spending all her time either with or thinking about Pax. She texted Sofía, Lauren, and Jenna and said they should meet for dinner at Scallywags. At twenty after seven, they were seated at a booth in the back.

Evie felt like herself again. Strong. In control.

"This is better."

Sofía frowned. "Better than what?"

Evie shrugged. "It's just that we haven't seen each other as much as we had been when I was down here before—for Lily."

"Because you weren't dating the mayor."

She leaned across the table and whispered. "I'm not dating the mayor!"

Jenna held back a smile. "Just sleeping with him then?"

Evie tossed her hands in disgust. "It's more than that."

"But not dating?"

Lauren said, "It's just puzzling that we don't get details. Jenna tells us things about her and Zach. Sofía talks about Nate. And I chatter all the time about Carter. So what's up?"

Evie blew her breath out in a long stream. "I'm confused."

Jenna said, "Confused? That's promising. Normally, you'd have the whole thing compartmentalized and sorted…including how you think it will end."

"That's the point. Or maybe two points. First, I can't figure out what's happening. I like him. I like being around him." Staring at the eager faces of her three friends, she rolled her eyes and said, "And the sex is amazing."

All three leaned back with a sigh. Jenna said, "I knew it."

"You knew he'd be good in bed?"

"I knew he was making you happy."

"I'm not sure I am happy. Usually, I'm a very strong, in-control woman. Not that I'm not strong around Pax. I am. He lets me be me."

Lauren reached across and caught Evie's hand. "So what's wrong?"

"I can't figure out how it's going to end."

Sofía frowned. "Maybe it's not going to end."

"Everything ends."

Lauren said, "Hmmm. If you're so accustomed to everything ending, you shouldn't be afraid that this will end, too. I think the real problem is you don't want it to end."

Evie squeezed her eyes shut. "And I'm going to get my heart royally broken."

Sofía said, "Oh, sweetie. What if you're not? What if he feels the same way about you?"

"Confused? Befuddled?"

Jenna nodded. "That's the first steps of love."

Evie's eye narrowed. "Love? I've known this guy about three weeks."

"You also knew him all the time you spent here after Lily's funeral," Jenna reminded her. "I did say beginning stages. I didn't say full-blown love."

Lauren agreed. "It's only going to get weirder from here."

"Then maybe it's pointless for me to go through it."

"Pointless?"

"The big elephant in the room that no one is talking

about is that I have a life. An entire life…with a job…back in Philly. And Pax is the mayor of a town in Florida."

"Oh."

Her friends looked at each other. Finally, Lauren said, "We thought you were beginning to like it here."

"I've always liked it here."

Sofía shook her head. "No. We thought you were putting down roots."

Jenna said, "You might not realize it, but this is the first time you've talked about Philly since you moved into the beach house."

"You unpacked," Lauren said. "You went grocery shopping."

Evie's head tilted as she studied them. "I was in the B&B before. I didn't have a stove. No reason to buy food."

"True," Jenna agreed. "But once your father arrived, we all sort of thought you'd repack and be ready to leave at a moment's notice."

"I haven't seen my dad. Except once at JavaStop. And he raced out."

"Whatever happened to your plan to offer him money?" Jenna asked quietly.

Evie shrugged. "He hasn't approached me." She paused. "It's weird." She bit her lip.

"You're worried about him."

"No." The answer was automatic. Mostly because if he went to jail for something he did, that was nothing but justice. She never argued with justice. But something bothered her about it, about how he seemed angry with her when she was the one who had the right to be angry.

Sofía studied her face. "You're sure?"

"Yes." Her phone rang, and she almost breathed a sigh of relief. Seeing it was Sam, she said, "I have to take this." She pressed the button to answer. "Hey, Sam."

"Hey, Evie. Remember that dance I was telling you about?"

"The one after one of the million stupid festivals in Paradise Key?"

"That's it. Anyway, we never got a dress for me."

"I'm so sorry! I forgot I promised to take you shopping."

"Dad said it was okay to call and remind you."

"It certainly was because I'm looking forward to helping you find a dress."

"Good. Should we go tomorrow?"

"Give me a second." She glanced at Jenna. "Can I borrow your SUV tomorrow?"

"Sure."

Evie went back to the phone. "It's all good. What time?"

"Do you want to do lunch first?"

She laughed at Sam's phrasing. "That'd be great. I'll pick you up around noon, and we'll find someplace to eat at the mall."

She disconnected the call. All three of her friends stared at her. "What? I promised Sam I'd help her find a dress for a dance."

"You're driving her to the mall?"

"Yes. There are a few things at the mall I could pick up for myself."

Sofía shook her head. "This is worse than I thought."

"What worse? How is this worse? She needs help. I'm helping her."

"You're integrating."

"Integrating?"

"You're sliding into his life like you were made to fit a spot."

"That's ridiculous."

All three of her friends laughed.

"I have a job in Philly and a life there," she repeated stubbornly.

Lauren said, "Whether you know it or not, you're also making a life here."

"So now you're saying when I leave, I'm going to miss this place even more than I normally do?"

"Yes."

She groaned. "You realize if my dad hadn't gotten arrested, I'd be in Philly now, back in the groove of the summer charity circuit."

Sofía smirked. "Sounds boring."

"It's not. It's good for networking." But she suddenly realized she hadn't even thought about it enough to send donations to the charities she supported. She'd fix that easily with a check. But recognizing she hadn't missed the charity ball circuit threw her for a loop.

And made her wonder if they weren't right. Was she integrating? Because if she was, that was bad. Very bad. As it was, she'd be heartbroken when she and Pax parted ways. But if she really was becoming part of this community, part of his life, returning to Philly would be lonely...

As lonely as every time she recognized she was going home to a cold house and a father who wouldn't talk to her.

SHOPPING WITH SAM threw Evie into a state of melancholy she didn't think she'd ever recover from. How could she have forgotten about the charity balls? The dresses. The mingling. Chitchatting with some of the smartest, most famous people in the city about...

Well, about nothing. But still, how could she forget she was missing the highlight of her year? After ten years of going to those balls, choosing shoes and gowns—

Ah, hell. Even talking to Sam a few weeks ago about getting a dress for the dance should have reminded her. Yet, she hadn't even thought about it, let alone missed it.

When she returned Sam to her house, the girl raced up the stairs with her new dress and headed straight to her computer and Instagram to tell her friends about her purchase.

Evie sighed as she followed her with her gaze.

After she was out of sight, Pax turned to Evie and said, "What's up?"

"What's up about what?"

"You seem...not yourself."

"I forgot an entire charity ball circuit."

He just shrugged in confusion.

"I told you about this!"

"You did mention forgetting a dance or something." He waggled his eyebrows. "Because of me."

She sighed. "It's more than that. Every summer, there are ten charity balls. Two or three a month from June through September."

"Sounds..." He lifted his hands as if at a loss for words. "Expensive?"

"No. I never mind the money. I like being able to support causes." She pulled in a breath. "I totally forgot them."

PAX GRINNED. "I'M getting to you."

She only smiled. Weakly. Last month, she would have tossed her hair and taunted him.

"All right, I'm not a fan of fancy dress-up events, but I'm guessing forgetting to go to a couple of balls, though sad, isn't tragic. It certainly isn't enough to make you this unhappy. But you're unhappy. What's really going on here?"

"How do you know I'm not unhappy with you?"

"Because I'm dynamite. I'm fun. I'm funny. I can cook. I'm going to show you Home Depot one day."

"So you keep saying."

That was better, but her heart still wasn't in it.

Before he could say anything, Sam raced down the stairs, the bag containing her dress flying behind her. "Going to Amanda's to show her my dress. Be back at dark."

She was gone before Pax could even say goodbye.

"Well, that was interesting."

Evie smiled at the door that had just closed behind Sam. "Women like to share things like that."

And maybe older women liked to talk about the dresses they got for balls? Maybe she was missing her friends? But, no. Evie's best friends were here.

Before she could get a chance to say she was leaving, Pax said, "Let's go to Scallywags and get a drink."

She glanced down at her clothes. "I'm wearing shopping clothes."

He grabbed his house keys from the table by the stairway and herded her to the door. "Shopping clothes are different than clothes to get a drink in?"

She led him outside to the covered front porch. "Marginally. But there's a difference."

"I'm glad you know these things."

She swatted him. "Don't make fun."

He said, "I'm not. I'm trying to learn." But inside, he

breathed a sigh of relief. He'd talked her away from her sadness over not going to her charity balls, but he hadn't missed the melancholy. It confused him a bit because he'd been glad to leave L.A.

When they got to the street, he caught her hand. "What is it about Philly that makes you miss it so much?"

"It's my home."

"I thought you grew up in Connecticut?"

"There and boarding schools."

"And here."

"And here," she agreed. "But Connecticut only reminded me of being alone, and I decided I needed a fresh start."

"And Paradise Key reminds you of being alone?"

She winced.

"It's okay. I get it." He also understood that by drawing her into his life, he could help her obliterate that feeling. All he needed was time.

They made two turns, heading toward Scallywags. Unfortunately, Lorelei and Tyson walked toward them on their side of the street. If he nudged Evie to cross, Tyson would see them and know he was avoiding him.

And there was no way in hell he'd let Tyson think for even one second he was bothered by the little bottom feeder.

"Hey, Tyson," he called before the other man had a chance to say hello first.

Tyson said, "Hey, Pax."

They took the final steps that brought them together.

"You know Evie, right?"

Tyson leaned forward and shook her hand. "Never had the pleasure of actually meeting her. You're even more beautiful in person than you are on TV."

Evie said, "You've seen my show?"

"YouTube. Your station has a few teaser episodes there. I think they might be looking at syndicating you."

She laughed. "I doubt it."

Tyson gasped. "Are you kidding? You're fabulous. If they are keeping you out of Philly because of your dad's troubles, it's only to protect your pristine reputation so they can take your show national."

Evie blinked. But Lorelei slapped Tyson's arm with her purse. "Did you have to bring that up?"

For as much of a gossip as Lorelei was, she loved the people of Paradise Key. The fact that she protected Evie said a lot.

"What?" Tyson rubbed his arm. "The woman's a natural. I'll bet if we got one of Pax's Hollywood connections to check this out, they'd discover her station has been putting out feelers."

Half what Tyson said didn't make sense in terms of how television worked, but there was no point in correcting him.

Tyson pointed a finger at Evie. "You just have to be careful you're not seen with your dad too much. In fact, if I were you, I might find a new town to hide out in." He winked. "Keep that reputation pristine."

Pax said, "Well, we're off to Scallywags for a beer. Nice talking to you."

He pulled Evie away as Tyson and Lorelei headed in the other direction.

"You still have connections in Hollywood?"

"Only my agent."

"Oh."

"You don't want me to call and see if your station put out feelers on syndicating your show, do you?"

"No. That's not how television works."

He laughed. "I know. Tyson likes to think he knows a little bit about everything, when he really knows very little."

"It's why you beat him."

"Frequently, yes."

She was quiet as they navigated the streets. Finally, she said, "He is right about me and my dad, though. The station owner never said I had to stay away from him, but he did move me out of the show so I didn't become part of the scandal."

He opened the door for the bar/restaurant. "You have no contact with him."

"But we're in the same town." She thought about that a second. "This is one of those situations where people won't believe we could be in the same town and not talk." She slapped her forehead. "Oh, crap. Why didn't I think of this before?"

"Hey, if no one's found you by now, no one is going to

find you."

"Maybe I shouldn't be risking it."

"Maybe you shouldn't, but honestly, Evie, he's the one who should leave."

"It's easier for me."

Pax's brain worked a million thoughts a second as he tried to figure out an answer or find an argument that would make her stay, but he got nothing. The bottom line to his plan was that Evie wouldn't go back to her show, so none of this would have mattered.

Except she hadn't yet realized she wanted to stay with him in Paradise Key. And part of the reason she hadn't was she wasn't ready to fall in love. Maybe didn't even believe in love.

That was her dad's fault. Not something Pax could fix.

But her dad could.

She needed to have a conversation with her dad.

And she needed to have it now. Not just for her own peace of mind, but for them. He didn't want her to associate falling in love with him to unhappiness. He didn't want her to associate living in Paradise Key to fear of running into her dad. He didn't want her to associate her sad childhood to living with him and Sam.

Before he and Evie could have a real chance at love, she needed a clean slate. Closure. And the only way she could get it would be with a sit down with her dad.

Chapter Thirteen

"YOU WANT ME to what?"

Pax looked Finn Barclay in the eye. "I want you to go to the beach house where Evie is staying, knock on her door, finagle your way inside, and tell her the truth."

"Oh, no, son. I can't force a discussion on her. She has to want to talk to me."

"She does."

"You're not hearing what I'm telling you. She has to prove she wants to talk to me by coming up to me. Either here at the coffee shop or at *my* beach house. There can be no misunderstanding."

"There already is a misunderstanding. A big one. She's thinks you're a liar, a cheat, and thief."

"I am."

"No, you're not. Well, you ended up being all those things. But you started out as a man in mourning, struggling to care for a daughter. You made all the wrong moves." He held Finn's gaze. "But without your daughter's help, I could have made all the wrong moves, too. For some men, you and I included, trying to raise a little girl without a woman's help is like trying to climb Everest without tools." He pointed at

Finn. "You made mistakes I might have made."

"Even stealing from her trust fund? You think you would have stolen from your own daughter?"

Pax shook his head. "Who knows? The point is your motives were good, and she needs to understand that. She needs to be told you didn't steal so you could gamble. You gambled trying to keep her in the life she was accustomed to." Pax stopped and after a beat simply said, "Please."

Finn rammed his fingers through his hair. "I'll think about it."

"Think fast."

Finn's expression changed from agony to concern. "You got a vested interest in this, boy?"

"She's falling in love with me, but everything here reminds her of being unhappy. If I don't change that impression soon, she's never going to want to live here."

"Change that impression?"

"She thinks you abandoned her here. She considers herself lucky to have found friends, but without those friends she believes she would have been alone."

"She'd have never been alone. There were too many people at the resort. And, at the time, I thought being with anybody other than me was the best thing for her. That can't factor into her feelings for you. It's too far in the past."

"Maybe so. But don't forget, you came to Paradise Key and jeopardized her hide out."

"Hey, I needed a place to hide, too!"

"And your being here causes her to compare the way I am with my daughter to her lonely past. She's connecting you and me."

Finn gaped at him. "Isn't that a little bit like psychobabble?"

"I see it happening. She's even told me that seeing me with my daughter makes her think about her past without you."

"And the only way to fix that so she'll live happily ever after with you is for us to reconcile?"

Pax breathed a sigh of relief. "Yes. She's never going to want to stay here if the whole place reminds her of being lonely."

"And you can't move to Philly?"

"I could. But my business is here. My houses are here. I'm mayor. And my daughter is in middle school. The worst time to take a kid from her friends." He shook his head. "But that's not the point. I think that the unhappier she is, the more she'll talk herself out of a relationship with me. And she won't give us a chance here or in Philly."

Finn looked him up and down. Because it was Tuesday, Pax wore a big T-shirt, board shorts, and flip-flops. He wished he had on his mayor clothes. It wouldn't have hurt to show the father of the woman he was falling in love with that he had a job, a future, instead of looking like a beach bum.

Lorelei brought over a carafe of coffee and warmed up both their cups.

Pax said nothing and prayed Finn would stay quiet until she was out of earshot.

When she was gone, Finn straightened his shoulders. "Okay."

Pax's heart stopped, then sped up again. "Okay?"

"You look like a bum, but I know you're not. I also appreciate that you're watching out for us. So I'll do it. I'll talk to her."

His chest expanded with relief. Not wanting to risk the moment, he rose from his seat. "Thanks."

"Thank me if it works."

"Oh, it'll work." He knew in his heart her past was the stumbling block. In fact, he was so sure that he leaned down and said, "Come to dinner at my house tonight."

Finn tossed him a skeptical frown. "Dinner at your house?"

"Yes. Tonight."

Finn sighed. "Okay."

Pax nodded once and headed for the door. Finn had his reasons for being skeptical, but Pax knew Evie had missed her father, missed the life they could have had together, and wanted another shot. Even if she hadn't yet come right out and said it.

In fact, getting a chance to be her knight in shining armor filled him with joy. A happiness he hadn't felt since Elizabeth.

Elizabeth.

Her memory hadn't grown dimmer. It had found a place. She had been his first real love. He'd never forget that or her. But Evie was his forever love.

He paused for a moment and looked at the sky. "I'll always miss you," he whispered. "But Sam needs Evie, and so do I."

A breeze blew by, tossing his hair. He laughed. Sam might groan at his tousled hair, but Liz had liked his hair a little messy. She wasn't exactly saying goodbye, just stepping back to let him move on.

And he was ready.

PREPARED TO SHOOT that morning's video, Evie glanced up to see Pax striding toward the boardwalk. He wore a stupid grin that made her roll her eyes as he took his place by the kite vendor.

Just as Evie was ready to tell him to start, he asked Dave, "Can I borrow your sunglasses?"

Dave frowned. "A prop?"

"Just a little something different this week."

Dave shrugged. "Okay. Sure." He took off the black frame glasses with equally dark lenses and handed them to Pax.

Pax slid them on before repositioning at the starting point, but Evie blinked. He looked totally different in sunglasses, so sexy her pulse scrambled. Since their dinner at Scallywags, she'd thought about nothing but moving out of Paradise Key. She wanted to go back to Philadelphia, but didn't think that was a good idea. So she started investigating other beach towns. But nothing compared to Paradise Key. Like it or not, she was making a home here. And just like that, her mind jumped to her father.

The truth was she didn't want to talk to him. At all. And the idea of calling his lawyers and offering to pay his legal fees suddenly seemed like the right thing to do. She might have told Jenna it seemed cowardly and cruel, but he hadn't thought of her when he'd moved here. All he thought about was himself. Maybe it was time she think of herself, too.

Dave said, "Evie? Hello? You want to get this shoot moving?"

She nodded. "Yes. Ready when you are, Pax."

He took a breath, shook himself out a bit, then looked into the camera.

"Hey! Good day to you. I'm Paxton James, mayor of beautiful Paradise Key, Florida. If you're looking for a little something special to do this week, come on down. We have condos and beach houses for rent. Several bed and breakfasts. Plus, there are plenty of hotel rooms available."

He didn't talk to the camera. No. He seemed to be looking at her, talking to her. His smooth Southern accent wrapped around her as his swagger spoke of cool confidence. And she realized, right in that minute, that she wasn't falling in love with him…she loved him. She'd fallen so hard and so fast, she hadn't even realized it was happening.

As if he'd heard her thoughts, Pax's grin grew. "We also have a first responder's picnic going on in the park. Take a tour through an ambulance, try their four-alarm hot sausage sandwich, then walk across the street and take a dip in the ocean."

Evie stared at him. How could she have let that happen? But she knew. Being preoccupied with her dad, she hadn't been paying enough attention to how skillfully Pax was seducing her. Not just in bed, but into his life.

"We have two kite competitions, and if you're bringing your pooch, you might want to enter him or her into Paradise Key's Dog Show. Now, we're not like those people up North who want to see a perfect pup. Nope, we grade on sloppiest kiss, best singing bark, and weirdest facial expressions. So come on down to Paradise Key."

He grinned, and Evie's heart squeezed. Hundreds of ramifications of loving him rained down on her. They lived in two different parts of the country. Her job was in Philly. His work, his *life*, was here. Philly was structure. Paradise Key was easy living, contact with people, a world very different from the one she'd created to keep herself safe and sane.

Even if she did bribe her dad to leave with the promise of legal fees, she hadn't intended to stay here forever. In this wonderful place. With this wonderful man. Eventually, she would be going back to Philadelphia.

"For a little downhome fun."

The camera rolled for another twenty seconds before Dave said, "Evie, don't you want to say cut?"

Evie shook herself out of her haze. "Yes. Of course. Cut."

Pax ambled over, took off the sunglasses, and handed them to Dave.

He faced Evie and an equally shell-shocked Samantha. "And that, ladies, is how it's done."

He bent and kissed Evie. "Dinner tonight?"

She could barely say, "Uh-huh." Partly because he was so sexy and so perfect she'd always be a bit tongue tied around him. Partly because loving him scared her, ruined her well-ordered life. If she stayed with him, she would lose a part of herself. If she didn't, the pain of walking away would be almost unbearable.

His smile was cocky. "See you at seven."

He swaggered away, and Sam shook her head. "That's his I'm-planning-a-surprise routine."

Evie blinked. "Planning a surprise?"

"He gets all smug when he thinks he has a good idea. A surprise usually."

Evie's chest tightened. It was way too soon to think he might be considering proposing…but Pax had never done anything she'd expected. Even as the thought of how roman-tically he might propose filled her with expectancy, the thought of leaving Philly permanently…*trusting* another person with her heart…just about paralyzed her.

WHEN EVIE ARRIVED at Pax's, Sam was racing out the door to have a sleepover at a friend's house.

Evie's nerves crackled with fear. She loved the relationship she was developing with Pax. But the thought of really loving someone, the way a man like Pax would need to be loved, terrified her. If he had a surprise that involved a ring, she was going to have to end it tonight. Which was why she hadn't cancelled their dinner. If he was going to propose, going to force her into the position of breaking up with him, it was better to do it now.

Her heart broke at the thought, but she reminded herself she wasn't lucky. She was broken. He deserved better.

She headed toward the kitchen at the same time that Pax opened the French doors from the deck and stepped inside. He wore a chef's hat and a big white apron over shorts and a T-shirt and looked like someone from a bad episode of a cooking show.

Oh, she hoped he wasn't planning to propose. If she could get her dad to leave, they could still have their fun, flirty, oh-so-happy fling.

He set a bowl of barbeque sauce on the big center island, walked over, put his hands on her shoulders, and kissed her. His mouth moved over hers with an expertise that weakened her knees. When he pulled back and smiled, it took her a few seconds to remember her full name.

"I have a couple of surprises tonight."

All her positive thoughts flew out the window. "Surprises?"

"Yes. I'm making my world-famous ribs."

"World famous?"

"I've entered them in contests from here to Tallahassee."

She rolled her eyes at the boast. He was back to being silly, frivolous. She could relax and enjoy dinner before she had to worry. "So, they're famous in Florida."

"I've been told the recipe got around."

She laughed. "You're an idiot." This was the man she needed. The one with the uncomplicated way of looking at life. Not the one fiercely protecting his daughter. Not the one who ran an entire town. Not the one who really seemed to want her in his life. The one who loved to tease and cook and make love.

And if she could get her dad to move, she potentially had an entire year before her dad's case went to trial. As long as Pax didn't do something serious like propose, they had a year of being together. A whole year of joking with him, being part of his life with Sam, and delicious sex.

He smacked a quick kiss on her mouth. "Get the wine. I smell sauce burning."

It registered that he'd only told her about his world-famous ribs, but he'd said he had a couple of surprises. Given that he was being so silly, wasn't nervous or anxious, she shrugged it off as she grabbed a nice bottle of red wine and two glasses and headed out to the deck. His second surprise wouldn't be much of a surprise, if he'd told her.

He glanced at the two glasses in her hand as she noticed there were three places set at the table.

"We're having company?"

"It's the other half of the surprise."

"So your daughter's having an overnighter and your surprise is ribs and company? Not a night of fooling around?"

"Company's not staying the night." He kissed her. "But you are."

Her knees weakened again, and she wondered why she'd jumped to the conclusion he was about to propose from one throw-away comment Sam had made. Sure, he seemed like the kind of guy who would want to settle down and she *was* nervous about her own feelings for him. They were deeper and stronger than anything she'd ever felt for anyone else. But that didn't mean he was going to propose—

Though, come to think about it, she had no idea who he'd invite to have dinner with them. One person. Not another couple—

"Hello, Evie."

Oh, dear God. Her dad?

She spun on Pax. "You want me to have dinner with my dad?"

"He's looking at the possibility of spending a decade in

jail. There are some things he needs to say to you. Some things I think you need to hear."

And this was why she didn't like serious relationships. Real partners had a stake in their other half's life, and they felt they had a right to interfere in their problems. No one interfered in her life. Her dad had had control when she was young, and he'd abused it. There was no way in hell she'd cede control again. Not even to Pax.

"*You* think I need to hear?"

"He told me the story behind—"

Fury rolled through her. Not only had he overstepped his boundaries, but he'd been interfering all along without even a hint to her of what he was doing. "You've been talking to him?"

"Once or twice."

"Both times my fault," her dad put in. "Once while having coffee by myself, I all but begged him to join me."

Evie glanced at her father then back at Pax. "My father cheated me, lied to me, stole from me. I should have had him arrested. Instead, I chose to protect myself by staying away from him. What part of protect myself do you not understand?"

"Evie, you saw how confused I was with Sam. Your dad fought the same battles. He didn't know how to relate to you. He didn't know how to talk to you. And he was grieving your mom."

"Which was exactly why I didn't have him arrested. I

gave him the benefit of the doubt. Some lenience. But I have no intention of acting as if it didn't happen. Not because I'm mean or bitter, but because I know him. You don't. Give him an inch and he will take a mile."

With that, she stormed past her father, running down the three steps off Pax's deck to his backyard, the sidewalk beside his house, and finally the sidewalk on his street. She was a block away before Pax caught her.

"I'd have gotten to you sooner, but I had to take off the apron and lock up the silver, so your dad couldn't scoop up a handful while I was gone."

"Don't try to be charming."

"Hey, you painted a drastic picture back there."

She stopped walking. "Yeah, I did. Because you'd tried to paint a really nice one with sunshine and roses and a dad who loved his little girl."

"He did love you. *Does* love you. He's facing jail time and just wants you to know he's sorry."

"I'll bet he is. He's finally getting punished for something he did."

Pax shook his head. "I think he's being punished every day. He misses you. He knows he screwed up."

Evie took a big breath. Her lips had started to tremble, and her chest filled with pain as the truth of their situation rolled through her. "You really believe that."

"Yes."

"Because he reminds you of you."

"Yes. That's part of it."

"And you think I'm wrong...closedminded?"

"I think you don't have all the facts."

"And that right there just proves how little you know me. I always have the facts. It's my job to have the facts. Your believing I don't makes me realize that all this time I thought we were growing close, you were doing what everybody always does with me. You think you know me because my life has been a matter of public record and you relate to me as the person everybody's seen on the news. The poor little rich girl who has crap for a father but drew a line in the sand to preserve her pride." She drew another breath, shook her head. "I thought you were different."

"I am!"

She pursed her lips. This was the other reason she never let herself fall in love. No one ever really knew her or cared to know her. They liked the shorthand version they saw in the news.

"You think that, I know. But you're not different." She closed her eyes, not sure if it was his Southern charm or her own desperation that had her believing things were different this time, when they clearly weren't. She opened her eyes. "I'm going home. Don't follow me."

"Evie..."

She started up the street. "Don't follow me. Don't call me. Don't send Sam."

The surf was high by the time she made it to her house.

Out in the gulf, a storm raged. She could see the clouds. See the lightning strikes. Another night, she might have watched it. Tonight, she crawled into bed, put her head on her pillow, and stared at the ceiling as the truth echoed in her head.

She'd never have a real life. Because no one would ever look past the impression everyone had of her from the press, from her show.

The whole hell of it was that she'd been the one to create the persona.

Chapter Fourteen

WHEN PAX RETURNED to his house, Evie's father was gone. He cleared the table on his deck, giving Evie time to cool off. Then he called her, but she didn't answer. He left a message.

He popped the cork on the wine, poured himself a glass, and sat staring at the sky as a storm raged over the gulf.

She didn't call him.

He didn't call her.

The night crawled on, a quiet, empty roll of hours passing. And he realized this was the rest of his life. Now that Liz had found her place and Evie didn't want him, a new kind of loneliness enveloped him. He was a single man. A guy responsible for his own life. Everything had fallen into place so easily with Evie that he'd thought himself blessed. Fortunate.

But, somehow, he'd screwed up big time.

By Friday, he couldn't decide if he'd been a sucker for Finn's story or if just by listening to it he'd betrayed Evie. But he hadn't known it while he was listening. It had all seemed so innocent. Still, he suddenly saw what Evie meant. Her dad had lured him in. Not that he was placing blame.

The blame went to him. She'd warned him her dad was a conniver. He hadn't listened. But her dad had coaxed him with a good story—a story close to his own—until Pax had believed he had to fix it.

Finn was the master. But Pax should have listened to Evie and stayed away from him.

He tried to call her a hundred times to talk this through, but she wouldn't answer his calls or return them when he left messages.

Over the weekend, he'd talked to her friends, who barely spoke to him, their loyalty to Evie obvious in their cool replies and refusal to say one word about her.

On Monday, he ran into Finn.

"That's Evie," he said. "Play the game her way or we don't play at all."

This time, Pax wasn't so gullible. "Maybe she doesn't like analogies that compare her misery to a game?"

Looking totally innocent, Finn shook his head. "Maybe. I've tried a lot of different things with her, but I've never really been able to get through. I thought this time, with so much on the line for us, was different." He sucked in a breath. "I'm never going to talk to my little girl again. And I deserve it."

Pax couldn't help it. He felt for the guy. He was a decent judge of people, and he could read nothing but sincerity.

Still, he didn't think Evie was wrong. Could this be one of those no-win situations? It seemed to be a problem for which there was no answer. A circumstance where everyone ended up hurt.

"I'm sorry."

Finn caught his gaze. "And I'm sorry for you. In trying to help me, you hurt yourself."

Pax said nothing. What could he say? He'd made a choice, thinking what he was doing would help Evie and ease the path for her to fall in love with him. Instead, he'd botched everything.

Sam raced into the coffee shop and over to her dad. "Did you hear Evie is leaving?"

Both Pax and Finn said, "What?"

"I'm not sure when, but at lunch just now, she told me that she was looking for another place to spend some time."

Pax stared at his daughter, her cheeks tearstained, her eyes red from crying. How could he console her? He couldn't even console himself.

She crumbled. "That's right, Dad! Just do nothing like always!"

Sam spun away and ran out of JavaStop. Pax made his apologies to Finn and went after her.

He caught her arm to stop her. "I don't know what you want me to say."

Sam's eyes filled with tears. "Say you'll make her stay."

"I can't make her do anything." And that was when the truth hit him. He was so accustomed to fixing everything in town, even the lives of his constituents, that he'd gotten overconfident and thought he could fix something no one could fix.

EVIE WALKED UP the steps to her beach house later that afternoon. She'd left her phone at home, so Pax couldn't get in touch with her after Sam told him she was leaving town. It was a coward's way out, she knew, but she absolutely couldn't risk that his charm would get to her and she'd settle for a man who didn't understand her. Who liked her persona and didn't see any deeper into who she really was and what she needed.

Just as she inserted the key in the lock of her door, she heard her dad say, "Hey, Evie."

She squeezed her eyes shut before popping them open as she spun to face him. "Isn't ruining my life twice enough for you?"

"I ruined your life once. I did a good enough job that I didn't think I needed a return performance."

"Then why come here? Why torment me? You have friends all over the world. Friends who could have hidden you! Why the hell didn't you stay away from me?"

"Because there are some things I need to tell you."

She clicked the lock on her door and stormed into her kitchen. "I don't want to hear them."

Her dad followed her. "This time, you will hear them. I

decided to turn state's evidence against the broker who got me the inside information."

"What?"

"You thought one of my friends gave me a hot stock tip?" He shook his head. "No. It was a broker."

She sank to a chair by her counter.

"The SEC connected the dots. And they were obscure dots." He shrugged. "None of that matters. The bottom line is they caught us. Well, they caught *me*. They need me to convict the people in the brokerage firm who set this up. They don't care about the investors. They want the firm."

"And you're turning state's evidence?"

"Yes." He drew a breath. "But not for reasons you think. Once I do that, I'm out of here. I will be free to go anywhere I want, and so will you."

She laughed at his audacity to think she'd believe him. "Oh, you did this for me?"

"Actually, I did this for Pax. The guy loves you." He snorted. "I think he adores you. But you have this thing about trust…because of me. I thought my turning state's evidence and leaving would do one of two things. Give you a chance to forgive him or give you the chance to go back to Philly. Heat over me turning state's evidence will die down in a few weeks. Probably two. Once I do a deposition and the broker is arrested, you can go home. And Pax can start the process of healing and forgetting you."

She licked her suddenly dry lips. The thought that this

could be over in fourteen short days numbed her brain. But the thought of Pax forgetting her shredded her heart.

"You don't want to go home, do you?"

She blinked back tears that should have been tears of joy but were tears of absolute sorrow. "I have to go home."

"No, you don't. Evie, when your mother died, I was so sure I had to raise you the way your mom and I had planned to raise you…with money and fancy schools…in New England…in that huge money pit of a house in Connecticut, that I moved heaven and earth to do it and I ended up ruining both of our lives. If I'd just looked at my own bank account, my own abilities…and what I really wanted instead of what I thought I was supposed to do…things would have been very different. Instead of trying to scrape together money to keep you in the house I lost anyway, I could have been making movies, making money, and making decisions about us that would have made sense."

"You'd have raised me in Hollywood?"

He shrugged. "Probably L.A."

"I might have met Pax." She glanced over and caught his gaze. "His mom was in a sitcom."

Finn sniffed. "Back in the day, movie stars didn't mix with TV people."

She laughed, but her eyes filled with tears again. The sound of her father's normal voice touched her heart, but the sincerity she heard there melted it. He'd never really been comfortable in her mom and grandfather's world, but he had known her mom would have wanted her raised in Connecticut.

And he'd tried to the point of ruining himself.

She could see Pax doing that. Not that he would have stolen from Sam, but Pax would have done anything to keep her happy, to keep his promises to Elizabeth about how Sam would have been raised. Because that was what grief did. It magnified everything. Especially promises.

And she suddenly realized it wasn't wrong.

Her dad wasn't wrong. He'd been grieving.

She squeezed her eyes shut. "I'm so sorry."

Her dad sniffed. "You're apologizing to me?"

"By the time I finished college, I'd endured ten years of pain. So much that it never occurred to me there could have been another side."

"It's difficult to think of 'another side' to stealing."

"You were trying to keep my life the way Mom would have wanted it."

"Grief's a funny thing. I got it in my head I had to do what she wanted, or it would be a sign I hadn't loved her enough."

"Oh, Dad. You loved her. I saw that every day."

He peeked over at her. "We had some wonderful times as a family."

"That was what I missed." Her heart hurt. Talking to him brought it all back. The Sunday brunches where her mom made pancakes, waffles, or crepes. The way one of her parents always picked her up from school, rather than a driver. The Christmases.

"I missed the Christmases the most."

"I wish I could go back in time and change things."

"I think if we could both go back in time, we'd make it so Mom didn't die."

"She was a wonderful woman. I adored her." His eyes sparkled with unshed tears. "I never even tried to replace her."

"I heard you asked Dotty out."

He laughed through his tears. "And almost had dinner with her and her husband."

Evie giggled, her tears falling so hard now she could barely breathe. She and her dad were six feet apart, but it felt like an ocean of time and space had disappeared in one short conversation.

He turned to her.

And the next thing Evie knew, they were in each other's arms, sobbing.

He said he was sorry a million times. So did she. As a grieving child, she'd been hurt because she didn't understand. But the adult in her, the one who always had to have all the facts, hadn't once considered there might have been another way to look at those facts.

Finally, he pulled away and said, "I will never, ever hurt you again. Once my testimony is over, I intend to disappear in Europe."

It seemed wrong to lose him when she'd only found him again. "You can't move to Philly?"

He smiled. "You think you'll be living in Philly?"

"You said I could go back."

"Oh, you can. The question is, do you want to?"

"Of course I want to! My work is there." She headed for the coffeemaker to make them both a much-needed cup of coffee. "Do you still take yours black?"

"Yes. But don't try to avoid the subject. Your work might be in Philly, but your life is here."

"My life is there."

"Your friends are here."

"I'm working on a plan to get them to visit me once a year, and I intend to spend a week here in the summer and a weekend every three months."

"You really can't be this clueless. The mayor loves you, and you love him, too."

She'd thought he loved her enough that she'd worried he would propose. A person didn't change that kind of opinion overnight. "He might surface love me, but he doesn't know the real me." She paused. "No one does."

"Oh, sweetie. He does."

"He can't, or he wouldn't have set up the meeting with you."

Her dad guffawed. "Seriously? You're going with that?"

Her brow furrowed. "What's that supposed to mean?"

"In ten minutes of honest conversation, you and I realized our mistakes and forgave each other. The day he invited me to dinner, he told me this would happen. He told me you missed me. He told me we needed a chance to make up for the time we'd lost because I hadn't been able to communicate with you."

Her breath stopped as she thought all that through.

"He didn't arbitrarily think it would be fun and convenient to have us both to dinner. He knew this would happen. He told me. Because he knows you."

Something inside her stirred. Something she'd never felt before. A thick, powerful trust. Or maybe a knowing. Not just that Pax was an honorable man, but that they understood each other and were people who could have a deep, honest love.

"I think I'd better go find him."

"I think you should, too." Her dad made a shooing motion when she hesitated at the door. "Once I drink my coffee, I'll let myself out."

She nodded and flew out the door. Urgency filled her. Not just a fear that she'd hurt him, but also her own heart hurt. She'd finally found the love of her life, and she'd dumped him.

She raced up the streets to Paxton Properties, then the mayor's office in town hall, but didn't find him. He wasn't at JavaStop or shopping with Sam.

Sam!

Tonight was the dance. She'd be getting dressed about

now. How could Evie have forgotten? Worse, Sam had come to her that afternoon. Instead of giving Sam time to remind her that she needed help getting dressed, Evie had told her she was leaving town.

She'd hurt both of members of the James family, and there was very little chance she'd be able to make it up to either of them.

An idea struck. A brilliant one if she did say so herself. She pulled out her cell phone and called Lauren.

"Who do you use for makeup and hair for your commercials?"

"There's a girl two towns up, Angie Perkins."

"Can she be here in ten minutes?"

Lauren laughed. "First off, her drive is twenty minutes. Second, she might have clients."

"I'll give her a thousand dollars."

"She'll be there in fifteen."

Evie hung up the phone. She headed to the Victorian and knocked, but no one answered. She tried the door and it opened, so she stepped inside and called up the stairs, "Sam? Pax?"

The house stayed quiet. No answer to her call. No footsteps upstairs.

Fear pummeled her. What if she'd done irreparable damage? Damage that no amount of money could fix?

Oh, she was so stupid! So wrong.

What if Sam had run away? What if Pax was out frantically searching for her?

Pax appeared at the top of the stairs. "Evie?"

Her heart about exploded with relief. "Hey."

"What are you doing here?"

"I made a mistake."

Clearly relieved, Pax started down the stairs. "I'm glad you realized you forgot Sam's dance. I am absolutely no help with hair and makeup. And accessories?" He took the last few steps and stood in front of her. "Who knew she'd need a special purse for a dance?"

"I did," Evie said, eagerly studying his face as she tried to figure out what to say. "But the mistake I was talking about wasn't forgetting Sam. Though that was a big mistake, too. We need to talk about us first."

He stepped back. "Don't worry. I got the picture loud and clear. If not from the way you left me the night I invited your dad to eat with us, then from the way you shut me out." He glanced away and swallowed hard before he said, "I can take a hint."

"I'm sorry."

"Oh, I'm a grown man. I'll heal. Eventually."

"No. I'm sorry for more than the way I left things. I'm sorry I hurt you. Sorry I didn't see that you were trying to fix things. Sorry I didn't realize you were right."

"What?" He frowned at her. "I was right?"

"Yes."

"Wow. What was I right about?"

"My dad." She sucked in a breath. "And me. We did need to talk. And I did want him back in my life."

His face shifted from confused to happy. "Oh, Evie. You talked with your dad?"

She nodded. It was just like Pax to forget himself, his own pain, and focus on her. How could she have been so stupid as to doubt him?

"We didn't get into details of our estrangement, of all the years of little hurts each of us inflicted, but I saw the big picture. Maybe because I'm an adult, I could finally understand his grief and his motives. He wasn't an excessive spender, trying to live the high life. He was trying to give me the life my mother wanted me to have."

Pax caught her hands and kissed the knuckles. "I'm so glad you worked all this out."

The touch of his lips to her skin sent prickles of sensation up her arms. She tilted her head. "So how angry are you with me?"

"Angry?"

"You did something nice for me and I threw it back in your face."

"Out of confusion."

She nodded. "True."

He waited a second—probably to see if she'd elaborate. When she didn't, he said, "Haven't you ever had a problem before that you worked out with someone?"

"At WKPP, sure."

"But as soon as you hit a problem in a romance, you broke up?"

She shrugged and looked away. "In fairness, I let the little problems slide and didn't break up until we hit a big one."

"Like people letting you down?"

She swallowed. "I see now I had high expectations that no one could seem to meet."

"Ah."

"I'm changing that."

He laughed and stepped close to her, dropping her hands so he could slide his arms around her waist. "Are you?"

She stared into his eyes. "Not because you didn't meet expectations, but because I think I might have made an ass of myself by getting angry about you inviting my dad to dinner."

"Keep going."

She sucked in a breath. "Then I wouldn't take your calls. I made it impossible for you to get in touch with me." She squeezed her eyes shut before continuing. "I thought I was protecting myself. All I've ever done is protect myself. All I know how to do is to protect myself."

"And now you see you went too far by never really giving a romance a chance?"

"No, the other guys were pretty much jerks."

He burst out laughing.

"Seriously, I was right to protect myself. But I've made

such a habit of it that I almost lost you."

"Who says you haven't?"

Her heart stopped. "I have? I've lost you?"

"No, silly! Life isn't about perfection. Nobody's perfect. I make mistakes. You obviously make tons of mistakes."

She playfully swatted him.

"We had some stuff we had to work through, too. Do you think you're the first person to offer to help me with Sam?"

Her forehead wrinkled.

"No. You're just the first woman I trusted enough to let into our lives. And you did a wonderful job. But whether you saw it or not, I only let you in little by little as I learned to trust you. And you had to learn to trust again, too. But it never would have stuck if you hadn't first settled things with your dad."

"We have settled things."

He nipped a kiss on her lips. "That's good."

She stood on her tiptoes and kissed him for real, enjoying the rush of freedom that fizzed through her blood. He liked her. She liked him. They weren't just lovers. They were building bonds of trust.

"Hey, people!" Sam's voice came rolling down the stairway. "I'm the one going to her first dance. You two can kiss while I'm gone if you want. Let's get me dressed!"

Laughing, Evie pulled away just as there was a knock on the front door. "I have a surprise for Sam."

She opened the door to find a blue-haired, twenty-something woman who, Evie was sure, Sam would totally relate to.

"Angie?"

"I understand I'm to help with hair and makeup for a first dance?"

"Yes. I'll take you upstairs and introduce you." She turned to Pax. "Duty calls."

"Better you than me."

She traced his lips with her index finger, as if memorizing them for future reference. "Why don't you chill a bottle of wine and order us a pizza?"

"Get the darned pizza, Dad. We've got work to do up here."

Pax laughed. "Okay, Sam." He smacked a kiss on Evie's lips. "You know that once we get her dressed and out the door, she'll be gone for at least three hours."

"That sound like just about the amount of time we'll need."

"Need?"

"I think I should make up for the week we lost."

A devilish light filled his eyes. "So do I."

Evie led Angie up the stairs and introduced her to Sam, who screamed with excitement when she saw Angie's blue hair and nose ring. They chose a flattering hairstyle for Sam's dark hair, made up her face, and slid her into the dress they'd chosen a few weeks before.

When she came downstairs, Pax's eyes filled with tears that shimmered on his eyelids through a few pictures and the arrival of Taylor's dad to pick up Sam to shuttle the group of giggling girls to their first dance.

Evie soaked it all in, planning to do a detailed journal entry so none of them could forget Evie's first official act as Sam's stepmom and Pax's soon-to-be wife.

Epilogue

TWO MONTHS LATER, Evie looked at the feed of the video being shot by Dave's camera and streamed to her phone.

Pax's face smiled up at her. "Hi, I'm Paxton James, mayor of Paradise Key, Florida, the best small town in the world. This week, the circus is coming to town. That's right. There'll be a big top set up on the fairgrounds. After a day of fun in the sun, you can take your kids to the show or ride the rides while you indulge in cotton candy and funnel cakes made right before your eyes."

Samantha peeked out from behind him. "Or not."

Pax slipped to the left, out of the shot, and Sam pointed to a pavilion. Dave got the shot and then brought the camera back to Sam. "If you're a little older and don't want to spend your entire vacation with your mom and dad, the Rotary is sponsoring this week's session of Band on the Beach, featuring Ugly Bananas. Come barefoot and dance in the sand."

Finn gently pushed Sam to the left. "Unless you like something a little more adult. The Wine Factory will be hosting a seniors-only wine tasting. From four to six o'clock on Friday night, we'll mingle. Once everyone's a bit relaxed, we'll have a speed-dating session." Evie's movie-star hand-some dad smiled charmingly. "Maybe you'll meet the love of your life."

As Finn shifted off to the right, Evie slid her phone into her skirt pocket and smiled for Dave's camera. "Unless you've already found the love of your life." Pax stepped beside her and put his arm around her waist. "Then, there's dinner and dancing. You have your choice of restaurants and type of dancing. So, come on down to Paradise Key, Flori-da."

Finn stepped beside Evie. Sam slid in beside her dad and said, "Where there's something for everyone."

Dave said, "Cut." He grinned. "Fourteen takes. I think that's a record."

Finn straightened indignantly. "My part was spot on eve-ry time. I think if we each individually taped our section, then spliced all four together, it would be easier."

"But then you'd lose the flow," Pax said, clasping Finn's shoulder. "The ambiance of all the generations coming together to prove that Paradise Key has something to offer everyone."

Finn rolled his eyes.

Evie stood on tiptoes and kissed her fiancé's cheek. "I agree with Pax."

"Of course you do. The man's marrying you."

Dave finished packing up his camera, told Evie he would have the video in her email in an hour, and headed down the street to his office.

Sam said, "Anybody want a coffee?"

"I do," Finn said, turning in the direction of the street. "Come on, kid. Let's run, get there before your dad takes the best scone."

Sam went from walking to running and raced off with Finn.

Evie frowned at Pax. "Aren't you going to follow them? Try to beat them? You're just giving up on the best scone without a fight?"

Pax laughed as he slid his arm around Evie's shoulders and set them off in the direction of JavaStop. "Silly woman. I've already been to the coffee shop. I had Lorelei put the best scone aside."

"Really? You went to all that trouble for a scone?"

"Not just any old scone. The best scone. Priorities, woman!"

She laughed. He could tease all he wanted about priorities, but hers were firmly in place. She and her dad were making up for lost time. She had a daughter to help raise. But most of all, for the first time in her life, she had someone she truly trusted and someone who trusted her.

All under the blue skies and in the warm sun of Paradise.

Life did not get any better than this.

By the time they reached the coffee shop, Evie's dad and Pax's daughter were already seated. They'd added a four-person table to the longer table where Lauren and Carter,

Jenna and Zach, and Sofía and Nate sat enjoying a mid-morning cup of coffee.

She ambled to the table as Pax went to the counter to order their coffee. "What are you guys doing here?"

Zach looped his arm along the back of Jenna's chair. "We knew you guys always met here after the video shoot, and we thought it might be a good thing for all of us to do on Tuesday mornings."

"Meet for coffee every Tuesday morning?" The thought of meeting for no other reason than to see each other warmed her heart. She frowned at Zach. "Who's minding the store?"

Jenna grinned. "His new employee. A college kid in Florida for the summer."

Carter said, "Took him forever to give in and hire someone."

"Because I don't need anyone."

Lauren laughed, but Sofía said, "It's not easy for some of us to give up control."

Nate, Sofía's newly minted fiancé, rolled his eyes. "No kidding."

"Eh." Zach shrugged. "It's a few hours a week, and he can use the money. Besides, if he runs into trouble, he can call me."

Pax walked over with his and Evie's coffee and his prized scone. Finn and Sam made room for them on the table they'd slid next to the bigger one.

Pax set their coffees down, then pulled out Evie's chair. As she sat, Sam displayed her phone, showing Evie a new video she'd found, this one explaining how to buy the right bathing suit. Pax and her dad got into a discussion of rising property values in Paradise Key, and how this was the right time to jump into the market. Lauren and Sofía began laying out a marketing plan for the resort, as Zach, Nate, and Carter talked about an upcoming fishing trip.

Evie soaked it all in. The noise caused by the chaos of friends talking over each other. People reaching across the table to get sugar packets or steal a bite of someone's doughnut. The way everybody seemed to mesh without even trying.

Jenna caught Evie's gaze and winked. Evie smiled. After all these years, she finally had her family.

And a home.

The End

The Paradise Key Series

After the sudden death of one of their friends, four single women who spent their summers at a beachside resort with their families return. The place they loved when they were young is falling apart, as are the lives of the four women. They each have their own reasons for returning, and their own secrets to keep. But as they bond together to restore a bit of their past, they find love in the beachside town, and the happiness they have sought all their lives.

Book 1: *Summer Love: Take Two* by Shirley Jump

Book 2: *Love at the Beach Shop* by Kyra Jacobs

Book 3: *Resort to Love* by Priscilla Oliveras

Book 4: *Small Town Love* by Susan Meier

Available now at your favorite online retailer!

About the Author

Susan Meier is the author of seventy books for Harlequin and Silhouette, Entangled Indulgence and Bliss, one of Guideposts' Grace Chapel Inn series books, THE KINDNESS OF STRANGERS and now a wonderful story for Tule! Over the course of her career, she's been nominated for and won several industry awards, including in 2013, when she lived one of her career-long dreams. Her book, THE TYCOON'S SECRET DAUGHTER was a finalist for RWA's highest honor, the Rita. The same year NANNY FOR THE MILLIONAIRE'S TWINS was a National Reader's Choice finalist and won the Book Buyer's Best Award. Susan is married with three children and is one of eleven children, which is why love and family are always part of her stories.

Thank you for reading

Small Town Love

If you enjoyed this book, you can find more from all our great authors at TulePublishing.com, or from your favorite online retailer.

TULE
PUBLISHING